MW00960282

At the Rumble of War
Neil Before God
BOOK 1

Ben Patterson

Praise be to the Lord my rock, who trains my hands for war, my fingers for battle.

Psalms 144:1

OPTIMISM PRESS

Cover photography by Woodsong Studio
Lisa J. Swartzentruber
Certified Professional Photographer
(302) 349-5956
e:woodsongstudio@verizon.net

Cover models are:
Taylor Patterson as Neil Avery,
and Olivia Massa as Ramona French.

Cover graphics for OPTIMISM PRESS
by Ben Patterson
Any resemblance to any person living or dead
contained in or on this book is strictly
coincidental. All persons herein are contractual
models or photoshopped and assembled parts
from various sources.

NEIL BEFORE GOD

Neil Before God Copyright © 2008 by Ben Patterson
All rights reserved. No part of this book may be used or reproduced in any manner whatsoever without written permission except in the case of brief quotations embodied in critical articles and reviews.

Printed in the United States of America.

For information address Neil Before God Books, Optimism Press, P.O.Box 512, Greenwood, DE 19950

ISBN 1-45368-160-4

EAN-13 978-1-45368-160-2

Patterson, Ben, 1957- present.
At the Rumble of War – Neil Before God/ Ben Patterson;
Illustrated by Ben Patterson

Summary: Life among the stars in the year 2235. Captain Neil Avery, a Starfighter pilot of the Coalition of Planets, had climbed quickly through the ranks. Trogs are everywhere. Killing them used to be easy. But every time Neil does his job, a little more of himself dies.

Can one man bring sanity to a universe where nothing is simple, especially when reason and matters of the heart collide? Not alone, he can't. Capt. Avery, a mysterious spaceship, and a one-time enemy Troglodyte set out on a journey of discovery, intrigue, and the hope of a new life.

At the Rumble of War
Christian Adventure Stories
Science Fiction at its Best

BOOK ONE
Neil Before God

BOOK TWO
Teri with the Lord

BOOK THREE
Doug in Deep

BOOK FOUR
Clay in God's Hands

CONTENTS

1	Issues	1
2	Treasonous Talk	5
3	The Albatross	15
4	Buried Alive	31
5	The Other	37
6	Detrimental Effect	39
7	It Is	43
8	This New Dichotomy	49
9	Compassion	59
10	Building Trust	67
11	In the Brig	73
12	A New Look	79
13	Getting Involved	87
14	The Unexpected	107
15	The Escape	109
16	Carl Ogier	115
17	Heaven's Mirror	119
18	The Shuttle	129
19	The Hospital	133
20	The Addict	147
21	The Friend	155
22	Heartbreak and Hope	163
23	Hope and Tears	167
24	The Rescue	179
25	The Answer	189
26	Terisa	203
27	Mr. and Mrs. French	213
28	The Awakening	223
29	A Plunge into Icy Water	231
30	The Wingman	235

Dedicated to:

Jesus Christ our Lord and Savior.

Also to Ramona, my wife of 24 years,
my eight delightful children who inspired this
writing, and to Olivia Massa.

Special Acknowledgement:

I would like to extend to
L. Claire Smith
special thanks.
Without her guidance,
and contributions to this writing,
this book would not have been possible.

Chapter 1

Issues

SO this is success?

Oh.

Super.

Tall, clean-shaven, and looking crisp in his forest-green flight suit, Captain Neil Avery checked his appearance once more in the mirror.

His contrived smile was ironic. Well, he thought dryly, I didn't wake up in a body bag today, and that's something.

He was twenty-five and had achieved all that he had wanted earlier than expected. A captain in the Coalition's Space Corps, Neil led the *Wolverines*, his own eight-ship fighter squad. But despite the prestige of rank and wealth, public appearances with fawning women on his arm, and *everything* else he had once considered worth having ... something about his life seemed woefully messed up, but he couldn't point his finger to anything specific.

Neil sneered at the image of the hollow man in the mirror, stepped from his private restroom, and pulled his helmet from his locker. Small hand-painted hash marks, each representing a "Trog," completely covered one side. Each kill had started out as a source of pride, but now the hashes served as a constant reminder: once done some things could never be undone.

Neil flung his helmet across the room; it

glanced off a wall, and brought the bookshelf down with a crash.

Immediately following a sharp rap on the door, Lt. Troy Younger peeked his head in. He glanced at the fallen shelves and the books scattered across the floor.

"You okay, boss?"

"Be out in a moment, Troy. See to the men, will you?"

"Excited about this mission, Cap? Man, finally something with a little meat in it. I'm—"

"See to the men," Neil snapped, glaring at Troy. "I'll be out in a moment."

"Yeah, sure. Whatever you say, Cap." With raised eyebrows, Troy withdrew his head and closed the door.

Neil considered his senior Lieutenant. He had managed to get his long-time best friend, Troy Younger, as his second in command, but was now wondering why.

While in their teens, Neil had taken Troy under his wing to help him get past a rough parental divorce and an abusive father. Troy was a year younger, so Neil got his friend into the academy by vouching for him. For the last five years they had flown together as a team. But in spite of their history, they seldom saw eye to eye anymore. Fact was, because of their friendship, Neil had turned a blind eye to what Troy had, over time, become. Truth be told, there were real reasons to hate the man.

The aristocracy thinks he's the ideal soldier.

They can think what they want, but I know better. If *that* is my best friend, thought Neil, what does that say about me?

Neil stepped to his desk, stiffened his arm, and sent everything careening to the floor. If he could have lifted the huge oak desk, he would have thrown it through a wall.

Appalled at his own uncharacteristic display of anger, Neil stopped. Get a hold of yourself, man, he chided himself. What's gotten into you? Where did this dangerous stupidity come from?

His mind panned back through the days and weeks in search of the trigger that changed his mood ... his outlook. Oh, yes, that new kid.

Carl Ogier—fresh and full of promise, an exceptional pilot, sharp and always ready—had joined them just a month ago. Even from the first day, Neil noticed that, no matter how hard he tried; the kid could never meet his gaze. It was as though something about Capt. Avery acutely disturbed Carl, as though the kid perceived something in his captain's soul that was ...

Neil couldn't put his finger on that either.

He dropped his head to consider the mess at his feet. To be honest, long before Carl joined the squad, Neil's growing anger started to take on a life of its own. The kid's boyish face—or the troubled look in his eyes—seemed to bring to the surface what Neil had, up until then, kept very deeply buried.

Avery's mind jogged back to the time he

first joined a fighter squad like this one. Just as Carl seemed now, back then Neil had high ideals; thoughts of changing the Coalition toward the better, toward a proletariat living without the threat of Trogs mucking about. But the more Trogs Neil killed, the more prolific the buggers became. There seemed no end to this enemy.

Problem was they knew how to blend into the population at large, making them near impossible to ferret out. Only eyes on the ground provided a sure way to discover who was who. This was exasperatingly difficult, though. Many once loyal citizens who had discovered Trogs wound up, themselves, contaminated and turned.

This next mission, tomorrow's mission, was designed to alleviate the Trog problem, or at least show them that the Coalition was serious about their defeat.

Still … that unknown something gnawed at the pit of Neil's stomach. One way or another tomorrow would change everything.

Chapter 2
Treasonous Talk

CARL OGIER wondered what this day would bring to him and his fellow pilots. Would *Wolverine* Squad see more of the same, just more killing?

Fully suited up for this next mission, he quietly shut his locker and tucked his helmet under an arm. The two hash marks on it—now painted over—said he found the very idea of marking his kills in this way, whether tradition or not, was as repulsive to him as the rows of tattooed hashes that spiraled around Lt. Troy Younger's neck.

Three hundred plus, Troy had bragged.

Sick.

Fighting a mix of acceptance and irritation, Carl sighed before turning to his boss, avoiding his eyes.

Captain Avery's manner and voice were always calm and self-assured—*leaderly*—but Carl hated looking into eyes that veiled all emotion.

"Geared up and ready?" Avery said, then turned away and headed for the situation room without waiting for a response.

"Yeah, sure," Carl muttered, knowing full well Cap couldn't hear him, nor would the *old man* care even if the words registered. Carl glanced at Billy, the only other new pilot.

Billy Taft shrugged and shook his head. "That old guy should retire or take a desk job. What's he now, twenty-five? Kind of old for a *Dart* pilot, don't you think?"

Considering Avery's replacement would be his XO, Lt. Troy Younger, Carl shuttered.

Younger nearly burst at the seams with a toothy grin. "Great day ahead of us, boys, but tomorrow will be even better. More Trogs will meet a just end. Yehah!" He headed out behind Cap.

It was clear to Carl that Troy was once again in his element. Murder came so easily for the man that it set Carl's teeth on edge.

"Freaky," Billy Taft muttered, referring to Troy as he brushed past Carl.

"Yeah," Carl answered, following him and the older pilots into the situation room.

Capt. Avery stood at the head of the room in front of a large computer screen waiting for his pilots to find their seats. Troy stood to one side.

"Get the animals fed?" Cap asked Troy, just as he had each and every morning.

"Yes, sir. *Wolverines* are ready, Cap."

The only chair open sat in the middle of the room, just in front of Lt. DuMass, Troy Younger's wingman.

Carl grudgingly took the chair. Any moment now Jessup DuMass would resort to his typical childish behavior. Carl waited for it; as expected, a wadded piece of paper smacked his head from behind, and Jessup chortled like a schoolgirl.

You would think that a man with as much gun under his belt as this one had would act like an adult, Carl thought. Well, there's one in every crowd. He quickly wiped the annoyed frown off his face, focusing on his captain.

Cap dragged a finger across the screen to pull a digital star map to its center and expanded it for all to see. With Parandi, the Coalition's capital planet, at its center, the map showed most of the surrounding star systems. Just four light years east sat its nearest neighbor, Atheron. Cap tapped it with a knuckle.

"Our target is a cruise liner nearing Atheron, boys. We've just received intel that suggests the ship, *Emperor's Princess*, is infested with Trogs. Key Trog leaders, actually. We can't allow the ship to make landfall."

Carl reared back. Had he heard right? "Intel '*suggests*,' Cap? Does this mean no one's certain?"

Cap's eyes, as cold as ever, focused on Carl. "The Consul has ordered the ship's immediate destruction before its passengers contaminate Atheron. Is there a problem, Ensign?"

"Capt. Avery, what about the innocents there? Are they doomed to die alongside the guilty?"

"Would you like to sit this one out, Ensign? No one will fault you—"

"Well, I will fault him, sir," Troy snapped. "If he has issues with the Consul's orders, Cap,

7

demote him. We fly *Dart* Interceptors; if he wants a surgical strike he can hoof door-to-door looking for Trogs under beds and in basements. I don't need anyone on my flight team hesitating in the midst of battle."

"That's enough!" Cap glared at Troy. "I don't fault the man." In locking horns with his first in command over this issue Cap was moving toward setting himself up for an overthrow. If Troy Younger was an ambitious man, and he was, he now had the means to usurp Cap and take his command. But Cap didn't show the slightest hint that he would back down.

Troy Younger hesitated, looking first at Carl and then at Cap, before restating his position more carefully. "Sir. With all due respect, we can't allow our men to 'opt out' whenever the mood strikes them. These orders come from the Consul himself. Consul Dais says kill, we kill."

Avery's eyes, once cold, turned hot with anger. "We're talking about downing a cruise liner, Troy, killing citizens loyal to the Coalition. And for what; a mere rumor?"

Troy's eyes darted around the room. "Trogs, Captain. We're talking about a threat to our society like no other."

"Really?" Cap looked at the map once more. "Have you witnessed firsthand the threat you say we face? Have you seen any real evidence of the damage done by Trogs?"

The room went absolutely silent. Carl and

everyone else knew that the lieutenant was Cap's close friend and protégé. A disagreement between them? In public? Unheard of.

Troy stepped closer and leaned toward Cap so as not to be overheard, but in the silence everyone heard Troy's low growling tone anyway.

"Captain Avery, you're talking treason. Calling into question the danger we face only stokes rebellion." He leaned closer to whisper, "We must take a firm stand, sir."

Carl considered Cap. What Avery had said was indeed treasonous, but his expression spoke of something more, something new, the least of which was rebellion. There was life in old Thorn-bushel's eyes, the likes of which Carl had never before seen. It was as if Cap had caught hold of a thought he'd only now considered.

Carl just had to stick around to find out what that might be. "Cap, I'm in. Sorry I led you to believe otherwise. Just wanted to make the stakes clear, sir."

Cap's gaze narrowed once again on Carl, considering him for a long moment before turning back to Troy. "Carl flies my wing. Reassign Tuttle."

Oh, man, thought Carl. Flying as Cap's wingman meant that on the way up to the transport, Carl was going to get a private butt chewing by Cap, and everyone in the room knew it.

Another wad of paper hit Carl in the head,

and he heard Lieutenant DuMass' chair squeak as he leaned closer to Carl.

"Now you've done it, runt. Cap's goin'ta burn you a new one."

After the briefing, Carl followed the others as Capt. Avery led his men to the launch bay to mount their fighters. They'd fly up to a transport awaiting them in orbit which would take them to Atheron and release them there in the morning.

WITH Carlton Ogier at his wing, Cap led his posse up in tight formation.

Carl tabbed the autopilot, keyed in Cap's *Dart*-wing code, and settled back in his seat to let his bird stay where it should all on its own.

Cap's voice crackled in Carl's headset. "What was going on back there, Ensign? At first, it sounded as if killing innocents bothered you. Care to explain yourself?"

"Yes, sir. If you please, can we make this just between you and me?"

"On my honor, my ears only, Ensign."

"I have my orders, and I will obey them, but to be honest it doesn't set well with me. I don't think killing should come as easily to a man as Troy or Jessup would lead us to believe."

There was a long moment of silence. Usually quick and decisive, this was totally unlike the actions Carl had come to expect from his leader.

In the silence, one issue nagged at the back of his mind, prodding Carl to push for an answer, even though his question might be over the top.

"Cap, you seem as troubled about the *Princess* as I do. May I ask why that is, sir?"

When Cap finally spoke, he offered only a hint of what was on his mind. "Hard to say, Carl. Truth be told, I was pleased to hear you question our orders. Someone had to."

Carl tilted his head back to stare out at the stars. The transport was still nothing more than a dot in the distance. "Do you see Trogs as a true threat, Captain, or is there something else?"

"Know much about Providence, kid?" Even through the crackle of the headset, Carl could tell Cap was careful to guard his words.

"Rumors and hearsay, sir. It's said Prov territory has been on a war footing with the Coalition for more than a hundred years. It's loaded with Trogs, they say. Why do you ask?"

"You say that for more than a hundred years they've held the Coalition at bay? Kind of begs the question, don't you think?"

Carl glanced to his left. Cap looked at him, but, even with the distance that separated them, Carl could tell real life now filled the old man's eyes.

"I don't understand where you're going with this, Cap. What's Providence got to do with anything?

"Chock full of Trogs, Carl. Chock full of

inferiors, isn't it?"

"Yeah?"

"Inferiors?"

Then it dawned on him. How could an inferior, any inferior, hold a superior at bay, especially for a hundred years? "Oh, I think I take your meaning, Cap. Trogs defy the Coalition as if they were an equal."

"You've got it. Intel seems a bit lacking when it comes to explaining that, but they won't give me any more to go on."

"Ever fantasize about crossing the border, sir, to see for yourself how they live … and how they die?"

Another bit of protracted silence filled his headset. Then a thought popped into his head. Sly old Cap had gotten him to lower his guard and speak his mind—speak treason. Had he been set up from the start, an elaborate ruse to get him to question the Coalition? Carl's anxious fingers strummed rapidly on his armrest.

Just ahead he saw the transport coming into view. Once aboard, there would be no escape, none that he would care for, at any rate. Carl got a mental picture of being shoved into an airlock, and yanked into the vacuum of space as the outer doors opened. "Accidents" like that happened all too often to be less than suspect. He took a deep breath, but even that was shaky.

"The truth?" Cap said at long last. "Yes, I have thought about crossing over, just to see.

Problem is, what if I like it better than here?"

Now *that* was revealing! Before saying more, Carl tried to quietly release his held breath but could hear it loud and clear in his own ears. Cap had climbed way out on a limb in trusting him. Although the desire to cross the border was Cap's personal secret, he would know soon enough whether Carl could be trusted with it. Treason was an ugly word, but if thinking for oneself, opposite established norms, was treasonous, then both Capt. Avery and Ensign Ogier were indeed traitors to their country.

"Cap?"

"Yeah, Carl?"

"I've got no desire to kill our own citizens. But I've got no out ... no solution."

"Tomorrow morning someone will die, Carl. It's just that simple."

"So it's them or me, huh, Cap?"

"Seems so, Carl. You're flying my wing, so if you don't pull the trigger, DuMass will take you out. You can count on that."

Carl didn't know what to say. What *was* there to say? Cap was right. Tomorrow morning, bright and early, someone was going to die. But did it have to be him? The only possible way out of this mess—*and live*—was to kill all seven of his fellow *Wolverines*. Carl balked at that solution, even if it had been possible. He was a good pilot, better than most ... but was he *that* good? He didn't think so.

The descriptive word for what he was thinking was "Turncoat," a traitor to everything he stood for; everything he held dear. The very reason he joined the academy to begin with was to protect these things. Now his own government had his back against the wall.

He shook his head in disgust, and then looked up to find Cap was staring at him.

"The question is simple, Carl. With whom do your true loyalties lie? With the Coalition proletariat, or with the gentry?"

With the people, or with the aristocracy? Carl's roots were well founded in the people, the commoners. But he had sworn allegiance to the gentry.

"The question may be simple, Cap, but the answer ... Well ..."

Cap's tone changed from grave to grim. "Now you see what I struggle with daily."

"Off the record, Cap?"

"Just between you and me, Carl."

"Looks like I'm going to take a bullet on this one, sir. Our motto speaks my heart."

Cap looked at Carl in utter dismay. The *Wolverine* Squad's motto was *Die with Honor*. Two years back, Cap himself had chosen the motto to show the spirit of his first and newly commissioned squad.

"Are you really willing to let Troglodyte leaders make landfall, Carl? The contamination would spread exponentially. Is there honor in letting that happen?"

14

Chapter 3

The Albatross

A MISSION. This is just another mission, Neil told himself to calm growing doubts, but it didn't work. He couldn't square the downing of a luxury liner on the mere suspicion that Trogs might be aboard her.

Had he retired a week ago, Neil thought, or even a day ago … this headache would have belonged to someone else, if it existed at all.

He released a long held breath. This was his responsibility and, like it or not, it was his place to make a good showing.

With his men lined up behind him, Neil started down the metal catwalk that crossed the spines of the *Darts*, all of his men displaying a stiff military bearing, but all the pomp and ceremony in the world couldn't mask what he and his *Wolverines*, were about to do.

As the march continued, each man stopped at his own ship. When, last of all, Neil stopped at his, every man turned in unison toward the nose of his own *Dart* and walked toward his cockpit. Once there, each man turned to face his ship with a singular snap.

"Wolverines," Neil shouted. "Mount up!"

Each man climbed down into his craft.

In unison every canopy slid into place, the bay lights went dark, and the huge launch door slid down, out of the way of the eight *Dart* fighters, to reveal the sun cresting Atheron.

Between Atheron and their transport sat the *Emperor's Princess.*

Sitting black against the dark backdrop of Atheron, the luxury liner was defined only by the light of her portholes, like strings of tiny pearls lining each of her fifty-two decks. Hulking and yet elegant, the sheer size of the vessel was spectacular.

She moved slowly as if to enjoy the sunrise, completely unaware of what awaited her.

Opening his torpedo tubes, Neil took a deep breath. "Show's on, soldiers. Slow and steady as you go." He jetted out of the bay with Carl at his wing, and targeted the *Princess'* engines.

Glancing back and to his right, toward Carl, Neil got a glimpse of his past. Looking to his left, he saw Troy, an image of a future that sickened him. He felt his face drain of color.

"Are you okay, Cap," Carl asked, still on Neil's personal secure line. "You don't look—"

"We needn't drag this out, men," Neil said, ignoring Carl's question. "Let's wrap this up before breakfast."

With sweaty palms, he rested a gloved hand on the button and pressed, launching the first torpedo. Seen only by its flame, the torpedo slowly arched to follow its target. Neil held his breath. The distant, tiny fire of the projectile briefly snuffed out when it connected with the *Princess.*

Then, all at once, huge explosions followed. The fuel and flame, ripping the luxury liner's engines apart, violently found its way into the oxygen rich environment of the *Princess'* interior, and burst from the portholes. Neil knew the fire that followed the corridors through the ship would instantly char anyone in its path.

Maydays came from the liner's bridge as the crew tried to grasp what was happening.

Neil nosed his ship toward the conning tower and released two more torpedoes, bringing the calls for help to an abrupt end.

The other pilots peeled away to target the escape pod chambers. Pods that managed to eject from the cruiser before the *Darts* reached their targets were shot down before they got far.

Neil turned, zeroing in on a pod as well. This isn't a military operation, he thought. It's cold, callous slaughter. He followed it down, but finding himself unable to squeeze the trigger, pulled up and away from the pod just in time to see the *Princess*, now unable to maneuver, kiss Atheron's atmosphere, tumbled once, then fall toward the planet as if sucked into a hole, burning as she went down.

While the smaller debris disintegrated in the atmosphere, the *Darts* followed this, the largest section, all the way to the ground. The *Princess* hit a farmer's field just south of Seychelles, burying itself halfway into the tilled soil, a massive clump of twisted metal and ceramic alloy. In all, from first assault to *this*, only a mere fifteen minutes had passed.

A PLUME of smoke trailing from space to here was all that marked a once majestic ship's closing moments and final destination.

Consul Dais had his kill.

Trogs, thought Neil, even Trog leaders, were they really so dangerous as to warrant this?

Neil's gut soured and lurched.

Suddenly a hardened decision flared in his mind. Enough! He was done.

As the *Dart* pilots landed nearby and got out to confirm the results of their handiwork, Neil followed in reluctance. He must have stood there stunned for ten minutes before glancing back over his shoulder.

Townsfolk were already starting to gather. Like him, they were shocked to immobility, they stared in silence.

Numb and moving on autopilot, Neil turned to the crowd. He wanted to say "Move along, nothing to see here," the standard Enforcer tripe said after each killing, but when he opened his mouth, nothing came out. Three thousand twenty three ... *dead*, never knowing that their government's sole reason for targeting them was based on nothing more than a rumor.

Nothing to see here? thought Neil. Someone should credit Consul Dais with what was due him. The decision to down the greatest civilian ship ever constructed was his alone, and he should get his lumps in the next election.

Moving in barely bridled anger, Neil spoke loudly. "Ladies and gentlemen, the dead carcass of the *Emperor's Princess'* is given to you by Consul Dais."

An abrupt corporate gasp faded into

whispers intermingled with weeping.

"Any complaints should be directed to Consul Dais, himself." There! He'd said it, fully aware that his words had just strained his friendship with Troy to the breaking point, greatly disadvantaging himself.

Now he needed to vanish, and quickly. Before he could make a subtle escape though, he had to "*feed the animals,*" as he liked to say; get his men settled into a filling—hopefully relaxing—meal. Like himself, Neil knew that his men had skipped breakfast, a usual occurrence for an early morning mission like this. He counted on them being hungry. And so, Neil reminded himself, disadvantage brings to light the more clever captain.

He headed back to where his men had congregated, and scanned the crowd. Ah, yes, just what he needed. Nearby he spotted a heavyset man dressed in a local diner's obligatory fry cook's uniform, a formerly white, grease stained t-shirt and matching apron.

Neil stepped forward, wrapped a friendly, but intimidating arm around the man and turned him toward the village.

"That's kind of you, sir," Neil said in a jovial tone loud enough for his men to hear. "Your offer to buy breakfast for me and my men is much appreciated. Lead on."

Without a word, the nervous man led them to a nearby tavern, the *Bush and Quail*.

As Neil and his men approached, patrons inside who were standing at the window staring in disbelief, moved away to resume their seats.

Even before they entered Neil recognized the fragrance of bacon, eggs, pancakes and ... what? He inhaled deeply and smiled ... toasted breakfast muffins, Troy's favorite. Good deal.

The door jingled as they entered. The place abuzz, suddenly fell silent at the sight of the pilots.

Surprisingly, the place wasn't just some hole in the wall—well, it actually was—but at least the owner had made an effort to bring in a little class. With mahogany bar rail and matching wall panels, newly upholstered booths and barstools, and paintings by some local artist hanging on the walls, the place seemed cozy, albeit just this side of obnoxious. This seemed as good a place as any.

Entering eagerly, his men brushed passed him to take seats at a large round table for eight tucked in a back corner.

Stepping into the room, Neil stopped to look around. A waitress standing at the counter caught and held his attention. "Ramona," her nametag read. At first glance she appeared to be an ordinary girl and he would have overlooked her if not for her petite, trim figure and brunette curls cascading to her lower back.

Ramona had just taken breakfast orders, and was looking them over before handing them to a beanpole of a waitress behind the counter. She looked up to see what had silenced the crowd. Then the young woman glanced at the pilots seated at the round table. But when her gaze turned to fall on Neil standing just inside the door, she frowned at him, and her unfriendly, dark, penetrating eyes revealed an unexpected depth of personality that riveted his attention.

Good, he thought. His men would expect him to smile, turn on the old Avery charm and—even if she was dating someone, or even married …

But the unveiled hate in her face hid no part of her feelings toward him or his men. Okay, he thought, I'll spend this night by myself, but if I'm to get away clean, I'll have to lead my men to believe otherwise.

Then he considered his options: Miss Thick-glasses Beanpole on the other side of the counter, a woman sitting alone in a booth—he shook himself. No, not a chance. His men wouldn't buy either choice.

He refocused on Ramona. Well, he thought, my ability to melt through ice hasn't failed me yet. This might be a challenge. I'll have to get her thoughts beyond what I just did.

Neil stepped to Ramona's side, propped an elbow on the bar nonchalantly, and said, "So—"

But she abruptly turned aside to take the breakfast orders of his men.

A sudden crash and clamor of pots in the kitchen said the cook was still nervous. The hushed, tentative conversations of the other patrons were beginning to rise again, but didn't hide their unease at the Enforcers' presence.

He needed a good distraction to cover his escape, but manipulating either waitress into helping him wasn't going to be easy. Ramona's quick exit managed to make Neil look, above all else, inept.

The officers in the back corner laughed and joked in an ill-advised attempt to make Ramona smile, ignoring the effect their obnoxious behavior had on those already here.

Neil could have left then, but for the longest moment he couldn't peel his eyes from her.

The waitress turned and noticed his stare, but made every effort to pay no attention to him. It was clear that she, in fact, found it difficult to hide her disgust.

Ramona handed the pilots' orders to the lady behind the counter, who shot a nervous smile at the captain before handing it to the cook. She knew, Neil thought. Everyone knew. How could they not? The *Princess'* crash must have shaken the place to its foundation. Who else but he and his men could be responsible?

Determined to steal the waitress' aid, Neil leaned on the counter beside Ramona to make small talk, but before he could speak, DuMass from the table offered an ill-timed compliment.

"Slick shooting, Cap. Bet they never saw your torpedo coming."

Without warning Ramona looked up at Neil, shot a thumb over her shoulder toward the pillar of smoke rising from the field just outside town.

"I thought that was your doing."

"That's the *Emperor's Princess*," DuMass said from the table. "It was full of Trogs ... but not anymore." He, and the men with him, laughed.

Without taking her eyes off Neil, Ramona's icy tone didn't hide her revulsion at all. "That was an unarmed cruise ship."

"Yeah? So?"

"Through its smoke you want me to see you as a nice guy, maybe go out and have a few laughs; take your mind off your job? Maybe even bed you?"

"Well, I—"

The cook slid a plate of eggs across the counter. Ramona grabbed it and swung it at Neil's face; its contents splattering all over him.

"You murdering pile of filth." She glared at him, then at the men around the table. "Take your business elsewhere," she said, as she stormed to the door. Swinging it open, she held it as if to send them on their way.

"Get out."

"They were just Trogs," Troy said.

"TROGS?" Her eyes shot knives at Troy. "They were passengers on a cruise ship; no threat to you or the government, fool!"

"They were Trogs," Troy said flatly, totally disinterested in any opinion to the contrary.

"Stop calling us Trogs!" At hearing her own words, Ramona's eyes widened in surprise.

Perfect. What Ramona had just blurted in front of the soldiers was beyond reason. If she had screamed "Shoot me! I'm a Christian too," she couldn't have implicated herself more. Unwittingly she had given Neil an opportunity he could easily leverage into an escape.

The whole room, tense from the start, fell gravely silent again.

Turning to the men, Neil saw that her words had struck each like a hard slap in the face.

Troy rose from his seat and slowly pulled his handgun.

Neil pushed himself from the bar rail to step between the waitress and his XO's gun, and pointed to Troy's seat. "Sit down," Neil said coldly. "This Trog's mine."

Spinning on his heel, he grabbed a fist full of Ramona's hair to force her into the street.

"This I gotta see," said DuMass.

Neil brutally yanked Ramona back, and thrust a stiff forefinger in the lieutenant's direction. "Sit Down! I don't need an audience. You think I want to kill her right away?"

"No, sir. I guess not," Jessup fumed, staying in his seat.

Troy smiled slyly, raised his hands in submission, and nodded once. "Have at it, Cap. Trog's got to be good for something."

"Give me twenty … thirty minutes," Neil said with a sneer. Fighting the adrenaline raging through his veins so as to appear unruffled, he drew his gun, and pushed her out the door. Stumbling, she would have fallen to the ground, had his grip loosened, but he yanked her upright, and shoved her into the alley beyond the sight of his men. She tripped and fell.

Slowly raising his pistol, Neil took careful aim. No matter what he wanted from Ramona, she could do nothing to stop him now.

Neil looked back at the tavern and saw his men staring through the window at him, and gave them a blatant brazen grin before stepping into the alley beyond their view.

Climbing to her feet, Ramona turned to meet him, fear in her eyes, but she raised her chin defiantly to face his gun with determination.

It was then that he saw her as if for the first time. The treasonous speech he had given at the *Princess'* gravesite was fully embodied in this Trog. The real threat to the Coalition wasn't this small wisp of a waitress. It was the Consul, old Ignacio Dais himself.

Neil stepped forward with, long, slow, strides until he was near enough to enjoy the color of her eyes. Returning his gun to its holster, he studied Ramona for a moment with heightened fascination.

"Oh, I see ..." she snapped. "Find it hard to kill someone when you have to look them in the eye, huh, coward? Got no stomach for killing face to face? Pretty easy when you can't see them, huh, tough guy?"

Neil's unwavering gaze didn't hide his amazement. She had taken a stance that Neil couldn't easily overlook.

"Thought a cruise ship was a threat, did you? Murderer!"

Neil leaned close and whispered, "You ought to learn to keep your mouth shut."

"Maybe I should offer my back to make your job easier." In defiance, Ramona folded her arms and turned away.

"You've got very little time before my men discover you weren't killed, Troglodyte. Time to head back underground, don't you think?"

She spun back around. "They'll kill you too, you know."

"They'll try, but not because I didn't end you."

Her jaw slacked in bewilderment.

Neil felt himself smile at this whole situation. Had she been at the crash site—*had she heard his speech*—she'd understand the irony. Like her, he had spoken before thinking, and with a word, sealed his own fate. Even before he walked into her place of business, he was a traitor to his leaders, and already dead.

"What now?" she said

"Your words have left you no way out but to run, Trog. I've given you a twenty-minute head start, so I suggest you get to it."

"And you? They will kill you too."

"That's twice you've said what I already know. Do you care?"

Ramona glanced away, clearly confused, Neil lifted her chin to study her eyes—she jerked away. "My men will have to catch me first. But you? I suggest you find a way off this planet before your own words catch up to you." With that, he turned and headed for his ship.

Ramona followed Neil to the end of the alley. "Hey, soldier, where are you going to end up when a bullet finds you? I'm not afraid to die for *my* beliefs. How about you?"

"If you stand there yammerin' much longer,

you *will* die for your beliefs," Neil said, as he kept walking out of the alley into the field. She followed him.

Before long, he came to his ship, climbed in, and automatically picked up his helmet from the dash. Moving to put it on, the little lines of hash marks caught his eye.

After a quick moment, Neil looked down, out of the ship, and saw Ramona standing beside it. "I don't want to die, soldier," she said, "not just yet. But I have no way off world." Her expression, a mixture of pleading and defiance, tugged at something deeper than reason. If he left her behind he'd have to add another detestable hash mark to his helmet.

Neil shook his head in resignation, and beckoned without looking her way.

Ramona scrambled up, and settled into the second seat, and then Neil fired up the engines. Although hers was hardly more than a jumpseat, it was still big enough for her slender figure.

"Under my seat, you'll find my spare helmet, Troglodyte," he said, snugging his chinstrap. "Put it on."

She smacked the back of his helmet. "Stop calling me that!"

He twisted in his seat to face her. "You got a lot of nerve for a dead woman."

She glowered, defying him to unbuckle her now, and pry her from his ship.

Neil clenched his teeth, turned back, and slid the canopy into place, then lifted off, knowing the scream of his engines would draw attention.

Troy would discover his deception—the missing body and no sign that the Trog had been shot or otherwise abused—and would soon find Neil's ship absent.

He knew that in their eagerness to skin him alive, his men would come gunning for him. But space and the ship he flew were his element. As always he felt his heart lift as his *Dart* shot up in a steep climb, but this was no target practice against an unarmed cruise liner. He was in for the fight of his life.

NOW chased by the seven other fighters, Neil's twenty minute, ten thousand mile head start wasn't enough when offset by the added weight of the waitress he should have, but couldn't, leave behind.

Stupid move, that, but it seemed very much in keeping with all the other idiot decisions he'd made over the last few hours. It now seemed to him that a body bag was determined to catch up to him.

"What's your plan, officer?"

"I'm no longer an officer, lady. The name's Neil Avery."

"Yeah, fine. What are your plans ... *Neil*?"

"Chagwa has an unmanned water processing plant. I'll get needed fuel there before we hop to the next system over."

"Isn't there a mining base on Chagwa's

greater moon?"

"Yeah, but it's manned."

"Yeah? So?"

"It's manned." Neil reiterated dryly. "That means *people*."

"But Chagwa's an icicle. I'm hardly dressed in extreme weather gear, sir," Ramona said snidely. "I'll be blast-frozen before you can close the canopy."

He rolled his eyes. "And that's bad … how?"

"Why didn't we just fly to somewhere else on Atheron?"

"The transport in orbit has each of our ships tagged and could track us wherever we went. We needed to get offworld and there's nothing closer than Chagwa. I simply haven't the fuel to go elsewhere."

"Hmm. So while your spacesuit protects you, I get turned into a popsicle. No way around that either, huh?"

"I'll defrost you. Now shut up and let me think."

"Oh, … peachy."

"What do you think this *Dart* is, your dad's skitter? I don't need to get out to attach a fuel line. It's a simple maneuver, a thirty-second hookup, then … with any luck, jumping from system to system, we'll get to Praxis."

"Where do we go from there?"

"We?" he said in irritation. "Beyond Praxis, *we* go nowhere. I, on the other hand, have a keen little fighter to sell to some pirate or slave trader. That'll provide *my* passage to Providence."

"What about me?"

"What do I care?" It was enough that he had to push his ship beyond its design limits to stay ahead of the others—beyond their reach— beyond their guns—beyond that waiting body bag. But on top of everything else, the dead weight in the back seat was now plucking his last nerve, and needed to be ditched as soon as possible.

A near miss flash said his men were nearing. Even with every gauge in the red and the small craft straining to obey him, his head start had ultimately given him no advantage at all. Every *Dart* fighter pilot in his squad, once a loyal friend, set Neil's death as his goal, and that of the Trog with him. Closing the gap, hours counted down to minutes, minutes counted down to seconds, and seconds to gunfire.

Neil tried to maneuver, evade, and dodge the barrage of bullets of his own men's guns as they, without a second thought, used all their skill to try and kill them, him and the albatross in the back seat.

Chapter 4

Buried Alive

HARNESSED into the jump seat, Ramona sat behind Neil. Although she couldn't see the *Dart* fighters pursuing them, bombs exploding all around Neil's ship, buffeting them like a pinball, left no room for any illusion of safety.

Knocked about, and unprotected by a proper space suit, the straps bruised and cut into her shoulders. She held tight, but twisted in her seat to peek over Neil's shoulder. Seven blips on the scanner said that, behind them, the *Darts* were gaining, but she couldn't tell how long it would take them to catch up. To her right, big and red, sat Chagwa's moon. The planet Chagwa itself was dead ahead.

With a rapid heart and sweaty palms, Ramona tried to hide her concern with a look of demure acquiescence—*in case Neil looked back*—but the muscles in her neck, tight and stiff, were making that difficult.

Neil had kept a cool head, but his own men hunting him must have terrified him, she thought. Certainly his years of experience and training as an Enforcer couldn't have prepared him for this, ungodly situation they now found themselves in. And although he said otherwise, Ramona knew he had nowhere to escape this time around.

She guessed that, with her added weight, he

had to muscle his *Dart* more than ever before. All the while in the back of his mind he must have known that once his own men caught up to them they'd see him dead.

The white snow covering Chagwa subdued her terrain, but it still looked rough.

He barrel rolled, dodged, and jinked hard, but still his own crew caught up to him, firing all the while. "I haven't taught you guys this one yet," Neil muttered. Almost immediately, his dart jerked into a complicated maneuver.

Ramona's heart lifted, and, for a second, she thought they just might escape.

It was not to be. One shot, one lousy little errant shot and his *Dart* jerked to the right, shimmied, and shook like a wet dog.

Just one shot.

His starboard engine spit smoke, burst into flames and down he and Ramona went, spiraling out of control toward Chagwa.

Ramona's heart was in her throat as the out-of-control *Dart* fell like a hunk of lead.

"Move!" Neil shouted as he harangued the controls. Still falling, the craft leveled. He managed to coax his ship into the atmosphere of the ice planet toward a level patch of wasteland.

If he could coax the ship to nose up just a little, just a smidge, Ramona thought, they'd have a chance. She hoped the snow would soften their crash …

… so they could what, freeze to death instead?

The friction of re-entry heated the *Dart's*

nose and the wings' leading edges.

Neil muscled the controls. "Move! Come on baby, up, already, pull up."

The ground rushed up at them. Neil held the controls firmly.

Slowly, straining under its own weight, the *Dart*, level on the horizon, began to nose up.

Too late.

The ground—

A sudden flash of white powder—

Then all went black.

NEIL AVERY regained consciousness. Light and shadow blurred in a confusing riot of images that clashed and divided and melded once again to form objects only to melt away.

Neil blinked.

The cockpit controls and instruments abruptly came into focus.

He looked back.

Ramona, eyes closed, reached up to a small cut at her hairline. Neil reached under his dash and pull out his med-kit. Snapping it open he grabbed a sterile pad of gauze. "Press that to your head, Woman. Any other injuries?"

She looked up, took the gauze, tilted her head back and rolled it to loosen stiff neck muscles. "I'll be okay," she said pressing the gauze to the cut. "Where are we?"

Neil felt his jaw tighten, and turned back to his instruments. They were growing dim but showed enough for him to realize his *Dart* was inching deeper and deeper into the ice. "Scanner says we're sitting nearly three hundred feet beneath the planet's surface. We're rapidly losing what little power we have."

Neil gave her a moment, but Ramona said nothing.

"Looks like we're buried alive. Some escape this was." He turned in his seat to see Ramona better. "Sorry, Trog. I gave rescuing you my best shot, but…"

Ramona glared at him. "Quit with the 'name calling' already. And besides, I wasn't the only one being rescued."

"Oh?"

"I doubt God's through with either of us yet."

Neil knit his brow in disbelief. "Still believe in this god of yours, do you? You Trogs are really something. Well, suit yourself." The thought caused him to scowl.

Although the *Dart* was buried in snow, Ramona's dark eyes were warm and intense as they focused on his face. "Until He's through with me, Captain, I'm bullet proof, and so are you. You'll see."

"One lousy little bullet brought us down, my little waitress. You're not bulletproof."

"Oh? Aren't I?"

Neil shook his head. "Look, there's one thing I don't understand."

"Just one?"

"Okay, several things, but one heads the list. Why didn't you run away? When everyone hates Enforcers, why did you come *with* me?"

"Not everyone hates you, Capt. Avery. God loves you more than you can know."

"That doesn't answer my question."

She diverted her eyes. "I was under orders to go with you."

Well, well, well … a Troglodyte spy had played him, and played him good. "You were under orders?" he said, guarding his tone. "Whose orders?"

Ramona hesitated. "Another time perhaps."

Neil reached back and gripped her wrist hard. "As a soldier, I understand obeying orders, but you better come clean, and I mean now."

"Ouch, you're hurting me."

"Trog?"

"I didn't have much choice. You grabbed me, then God … God said to go with you."

Great, Neil thought, a nut-job who hears voices. She seemed sincere, and that in itself was scary. Neil released her.

"So you will obey this god of yours in spite of any apparent danger? Old Consul Dais won't get that much from me, dreamy-eyed girl."

"Dreamy eyed?" Her words flared defiance. "Perhaps. But I've often wondered whether I would refuse the most difficult task my Lord asked of me. Well, now I know."

"I still don't see why you let slip you were a Trog when my men were sitting right there. Didn't you understand that as an Enforcer I was duty bound to kill you?"

"I knew." Ramona lifted her eyes to focus

on his. "It was a slip of the tongue, but the moment I said it, I knew it was the right thing to say. Some things are more important than life. If then and there Jesus hadn't told me to stay the course, I would've probably tried to backtrack."

One corner of Neil's mouth pulled into an amused grin as he remembered her in the alley. "It took courage to face death as you did, but where does that leave us? This god you're so fond of, is he going to reach into this ice and pluck us out?"

She tilted her head and her eyes revealed a glimmer of hope. "Providence, Mr. Avery; do you know what the word means?"

He did not.

"Well, *Neil*, it means, 'to be held in God's hands.' I *know* we're in His hands, even now."

Unconsciously Neil's brows furrowed more deeply as he puzzled at the boldness written in her eyes. "Well, I see no way out of this mess. I'm at my wit's end."

"There's a higher power than our wits, Neil Avery. Of *that*, you can be assured."

He considered the naked strength written in her face. "We're buried alive, little lady. My ship's power is near gone, and we'll soon be out of oxygen. I think your confidence is misplaced. Why do you still hang on to this god nonsense anyway?"

"I've found He's full of surprises, Captain."

Suddenly the ship lurched forward.

Chapter 5
The Other

HIGH overhead, above the snow and ice, Neil's chief Lieutenant, Troy Younger, circled the crater made by Neil's ship; six *Dart* fighter craft followed his.

Jessup DuMass' agitation showed in his voice as it crackled in Troy's earpiece. "Let's head home, boss. Cap's gone for sure."

"No, Jess. The Consul wouldn't want us to leave our Captain's life to chance. I say we go in after him; him and that stinking Trog."

"L.T., look at the size of that crater. No one could've survived that. They're dead."

"And even if they did," Ensign Hedges said, "they're buried alive and will freeze solid soon enough. Captain's ship isn't going to fly again. Let's go home before we run out of fuel ourselves."

"Stay put while we go in," shouted Troy. "Jess, you're with me. Overloading your guns will superheat the skin of your *Dart*. We'll melt our way in and make sure he's dead."

"What? Through snow and ice? Are you nuts, L.T.?"

"Watch your tone, Jessup. Melting through snow and ice is an old trick of Neil's. We'll follow him in and make certain he's dead. Now get those guns hot. The rest of you, refuel at the refinery. If Neil manages the impossible, I want you ready. Kill him and that stinking Trog. Am

I understood?"

Troy and his wingman dove into the snow crater.

NOSE down in total darkness; Neil's *Dart* was stuck solid. He hit the lights and saw that his ship was wedged between the wall it had just burst through and some sort of floor. It's nose had buried itself two feet into the ice. He only got a glimpse, but he saw that his ship was stuck just inside a huge ice cavern.

Neil opened the canopy just as the lights faded completely.

With his ship's energy gone, the craft was little more than a shell.

Ramona's teeth began to chatter. He fumbled in the dark for his *Survival Kit*, and by feel could tell that Joey had worked on his ship. That mechanic had a penchant for being ill organized and lazy. Joey hadn't restocked Neil's *Kit* leaving it with nothing but the one little chemical torch in the way of tools … no food, no water.

"Well," Neil dusted off his hands. "Looks like it's time to explore." By touch alone, he and Ramona climbed out and down to the ground. Aggravated by the lack of preparation, he sighed, raised the lone chemical torch and snapped it. Instantly a brilliant white light blinded him. When his eyes adjusted, he found the huge ice cavern already had an occupant.

Chapter 6
Detrimental Effect

NEIL AVERY stared in wonder.

"Well, would you look at that? A spaceship? Hidden here? By whom and for how long?"

Among the stalactites sat a pure white, 180-foot long spacecraft. Its luminous skin lit the entire cavern. And as if it had waited to welcome them specifically, the hatch opened, and the ramp lowered.

Hugging herself, teeth chattering, Ramona forced a smile. "My, my, Mr. Avery, it seems there's a God after all, wouldn't you say?" Shivering, she took a step toward the mysterious craft "I hope it's warm in there."

Suddenly the two pursuing *Darts* burst through the cavern wall with a crash, and slid to a halt a few yards away, scattering a veritable storm of ice and snow.

Stumbling, Neil scrambled to his feet, gripped Ramona's hand, and the two of them bolted toward the white spacecraft.

Dazed, the two *Dart* pilots climbed from their little ships, and came after them.

She and Neil made it into the craft where, tossing his helmet aside, he frantically searched for a button, lever, or control panel; something to close the hatch.

In the warm chamber, Ramona removed her helmet, and reflexively yelled, "Raise the ramp!" and as if in obedience, the ramp rose, emanating a mechanical hum.

But before it could close completely, both Enforcers scrambled aboard.

Neil reached for his sidearm. Strangely, his holster was empty. Now, facing his one-time comrades, he saw enemies.

Determined, they squared their shoulders, and each leisurely drew his gun. Troy faced his Captain with nothing but pity in his eyes.

"Looks like you found this Trog a pretty big coffin, Neil." With slow, deliberate actions, and smirking as if killing Ramona was going to be the high point of his day, Troy aimed his gun.

Instinctively, Neil stepped between Troy's weapon and Ramona once again, but this time he scarcely recognized his best friend.

"Out of the way, Neil."

"I've never known you to go so far for needless slaughter, Troy. Why so determined? How did you become so twisted?"

Troy's demeanor changed to one of disparagement. "Needless, Neil? Haven't you learned anything from history? Religion is a cancer that weakens the whole of society. It suffocates an individual's free pursuit of logic, science, and natural law. I don't need a religious Trog telling me what to eat, who to see, or how to behave. Banning religion has set us free, Neil. I thought you knew that."

Behind Neil, Ramona piped up. "I'm a citizen of this so-called Coalition of Planets, and I'm not free."

Neil glared at Troy. "The people we killed—those on the *Princess* who weren't Trogs—were they free? Come on, Lt. Younger. Who are the oppressors here, *really*?"

"I have my orders, Captain Avery. She's a threat that needs to be neutralized, plain and simple. I'm not going to argue points and positions that should be obvious to you."

"Troy, up to this point you and I had always agreed. Like you, I thought Christianity needed to be snuffed out. But with this last mission, cold hard truth slapped some sense into me. As long as the Coalition is willing to tear the wheat out to get at the weeds, no one is safe; not even you, my friend. Can't you see that?"

Troy's scowl grew. "This subversive, with a wink and a nod, has turned the most loyal man I've ever met against the Coalition, and you don't see her ability to do *that* as dangerous? Not even to the rest of us?"

"She didn't do that, Troy. Our last orders did. The Coalition has blurred the lines by lumping the innocents with the guilty. Why'd they do that? To maintain purity? Absurd. By ordering indiscriminate killing, our own regime has taken our freedom from us. The truly dangerous party here is our own government."

Troy scoffed. "It's her effect on you, Neil, that's got me worried."

"You want to take a life, Troy, then take mine. Just let her live."

Aiming his gun at Neil's heart, Troy's face was a mix of frustration and resolve. "Cap, I have no desire to kill you. None. But from this point on, your own words seal your fate. Because we have history, I forgave your treasonous talk in the ready room. And I held my peace when you spoke at the *Princess*. Had you walked away then, I would have let you escape. Even now, Cap, if you step aside, I'll let you go. But you're going too far in protecting this Trog. If you don't step aside, you *will* die with her. Don't force me kill my best friend too."

Neil gritted his teeth and set his jaw. "Those poor people we killed this morning did nothing to us. They hurt none of us: you, the Coalition, or me. So a few might have believed in a deity to help them get through their struggles. *Big deal*. Most of those passengers were innocent. Did they need to die with the guilty?"

Troy cocked his head to study his onetime friend as if Neil's views were unique and curiously absurd. "Forget all that. Why do you now protect her ... *this* specific heretic?"

Neil glanced back at Ramona, and then looked at Troy with renewed purpose. "Even if it's just one life, I'm done giving in to evil."

"Evil?" Troy spat the word as if Neil had finally reached that invisible breaking point. "Look at this, Jessup, and remember; Trogs have a detrimental effect on everyone they touch. See what this one's done to Cap?"

With cold eyes, Troy raised his gun and pulled the trigger.

The world went black.

Chapter 7
It Is

ON his back and dazed, Neil propped himself up on an elbow to look around but found he was surrounded by an eternity of white. For a fleeting moment, everything felt warm and peaceful, his fears hung suspended just beyond his reach, and he felt no pain.

Behind him, to his left, and looking as baffled as he felt, Ramona raised herself to a sitting position.

The two Lieutenants, now unconscious, lay a few feet away.

A soft voice seemed to come from nowhere and from everywhere at once. "Do you want to terminate these men, or shall I?"

Startled, Neil hunted for the voice's source but found nothing. Could *this* be Ramona's god? He gulped and spoke without thinking. "Me? Are you talking to me?"

"Yes, Neil Avery, I am speaking to you."

"Who are you?" he said.

"Me?" the voice responded.

Neil grimaced and cursed his clumsy mouth. That's right, speak without thinking and tick off some deity. He braced himself, half expecting to be struck by lightning.

"I am your ship," came the reply. "Do you want to terminate these men, or shall I?"

"Ship? My ship? What makes you my ship?" Neil tried to focus, but it was difficult through a mind as muddled as his.

"I have waited for you, Neil Avery, for you and Ramona French to arrive. And so you have. Now I await your orders." A pistol appeared by his hand.

Neil picked up the gun to examine. It was *his* Zithion blaster. He knew he'd lost it in the cavern, but now here it was, clean and ready.

The two Lieutenants, in turn, revived and sat up. Panicked, Troy jumped to his feet and searched his belt for his gun, but it was gone.

Neil, on the other hand, had his weapon aimed squarely at Troy's head. "Well now, this is an interesting turn of events, wouldn't you say, Troy?"

Troy raised his hands, and, after climbing to his feet, Jessup did the same.

While there was nothing to suggest time or space, Neil looked around in an effort to get his bearings, but kept his gun on his onetime comrades as he got to his feet.

"Do you want me to terminate these men," asked the ship, "or do you wish to?"

His words paced, Neil spoke with a cavalier attitude. "Wow. Seems my new ship has it in for you two, Troy. Why do you suppose that is?"

"These are evil men. They must be terminated," the ship said, its tone frighteningly matter-of-fact.

Disadvantaged, Troy and Jessup glanced at each other, neither secure in his standing with Neil, given what they had come to do.

"Funny," Neil said. "This ship sounds just

like you, Troy. It has determined your guilt without a trial. Think it knows better who should live and who should die?"

"If you let these men live," persisted the ship, "they'll hunt you for the rest of your life."

With a calculating eye, Neil considered his men. "Is that right, Troy? You won't leave well enough alone? You can't let us go in peace?"

The Lieutenant shifted nervously but said nothing.

As he adjusted his grip on the gun, Neil gave Troy renewed attention, and tried to get through to his one time friend again. "Given the chance, Troy, would you let us live?"

Troy straightened into a formal military stance. "I have my orders. Standing by her will guarantee your death, Captain. That's why I'm here."

"Well, that's too bad, Mr. Younger. You're unarmed." Neil turned his gun to the other. "Jessup? Do you feel the same?"

As if to find stability in this suddenly upside down situation, Jessup shot a nervous glance at Troy.

"Don't look at him, Jess. You live or die on your own merits. Given the chance, would you let us go our separate ways?"

Unlike Troy, Jessup began to sweat. "If the situation was reversed, Captain, would you?"

Neil considered his Lieutenants. Had this been yesterday, Jess might have been right. But this was a new day, a day full of revelation and surprise.

"It would seem that the only ones who want someone dead are those that lack a heart."

"But they will—"

"For starters, ship," Neil interrupted, "I'm not going to argue with a machine about life and death issues." Neil turned to Ramona. "How about you? You want someone dead?"

"Well, I—"

"If you let these evil men go," the ship insisted, "they will hinder your work at every turn. They must die."

Neil studied his XO. "Make no mistake, Troy. I'm no different than you. I taught you to kill, and the same blood—*Christian blood*—is as much on my hands as it is on yours. This ship, my ship, seems to have it in for you, but not for me. Why do you suppose that is?"

"Unlike you," came the voice, "their god is the government. Their god has declared your life forfeit, and you will not be able to return to the Coalition without great risk."

"Did you hear that, Troy?" Neil raised his pistol. "By this ship's reckoning, you have a god. That makes you religious, doesn't it? Should I kill you for that?"

Troy shifted and glanced at Jessup with uncertainty in his expression.

Without looking back, Neil reached out a hand and helped Ramona to her feet. "This very morning I was supposed to take this Trog's life, Troy, but I couldn't see how doing so served justice. Now I'm supposed to take yours. What am I to do with that?"

Troy slowly shook his head with obvious disdain. "I would rather have died than to see you like this, Captain ... weak ... pathetic."

Neil's unreadable eyes riveted Troy and gave him nowhere to retreat.

"Weak?" Neil mocked softly. "I have no fear of you, or her. Does that make me weak, or do you see fear of an unarmed woman as a sign of strength?"

Mouth agape, Troy faced Neil in silence.

Neil handed Ramona his gun, before stepping forward to stand between Troy and Jessup draping an arm over each man.

Ramona's voice was cold as she aimed the gun at the men. "While your changed outlook is interesting to see in an Enforcer, Mr. Avery, it doesn't seem well-timed."

"A Trog with a gun," Neil whispered into Troy's ear. "Who's scared now?"

Neil's helmet suddenly appeared between him and Ramona. At seeing the hash marks, shame and grief instantly flooded his mind. Did the woman know their meaning? Did she have any idea?

"I see the high count, Neil, and those around Troy's neck, and I know what they mean." Ramona's tone was frank. "God forgives you, and so do I." She lowered the gun.

"God forgives?" Troy spoke with clear contempt. "Who are you to speak for God?"

Ramona looked squarely at Troy, her eyes smiling, her mouth wanting to do the same. "You just acknowledged the existence of God,

Lieutenant, and that is a good start. There may be hope for you yet. I believe God has spoken. I simply carry the message He has given to all of those who belong to Him. And just so you know, He has forgiven you two Enforcers as well."

"This god you speak of," Neil said. "*You* may believe He lives and speaks, but don't ask me to buy into any of this religious nonsense."

"God is real, Captain, despite your belief to the contrary."

"If that's so," Neil said, "I should think your god would demand my life to pay for the years I've spent killing, and for the buckets of Christian blood on my hands."

"He doesn't ask for your life," said the ship. "He asks for theirs. Where does your heart lie, with her who forgives you, or with those who insist you die? Choose wisely where your greater loyalty lies. This may be the last chance to get it right."

Neil frowned, "Do you really want to know the limit to my loyalty? Then check this; if God requires a life, He can have mine. I was dead anyway."

"That answer is unacceptable."

"Then this is finished. If you're heart-set on killing someone, then you must condemn me, too. I stand with these men."

"Is that your final decision?"

Neil considered the others knowing his next two words would change everything.

"It is."

Chapter 8

This New Dichotomy

SEARING pain overwhelmed Neil's mind, instantly clouding any sense of his surroundings. Incredible pressure squeezed his entire body while every muscle felt torn, consumed by fire, blast frozen, and melting away, all at the same time. As though gripped by a giant beast, razor-sharp claws grabbed and flung him into nothingness. Tumbling out of control, all went black.

When he finally regained consciousness, he found himself in such tremendous agony he barely noticed the cold, hard floor on which he lay. He spread his arms and legs in search of something to grip or cling to, as the room rolled and swam, but his efforts were in vain.

His stomach ruthlessly clenched, churned, and tossed, refusing to settle.

As he struggled to sit, intense pain shot through his temples, slamming him back to the floor. He knew but one thing, could almost see it, really. Claws slashed and teeth ground, as death stalked him with plans to completely devour him if given the chance.

"NO!" The word burst out of his agony as Neil refused to give in to the torture or the bewildering confusion attacking him. Struggling to sit once again, he paused before pushing himself to his feet. Determined to stand, he swayed, trying to compose himself.

When his eyes adjusted, he saw Ramona lying near him. Though unconscious, she writhed and convulsed in her own internal war.

"I deserve this!" he screamed. "Not her! Not her."

Tears and sweat streamed freely down his face, as he stood there, defiant.

"For the sake of her love for You, God, stop hurting her!"

Then as abruptly as it had begun, the torture stopped. Exhausted and dazed, he collapsed to the floor, fading in and out of consciousness.

When his mind finally settled and began to function somewhat normally, he inhaled, but the simple act of drawing a breath argued with a deep-seated ache in his ribs. Although a struggle, his lungs still worked in any event. Was he still alive? Could he be? Could he have survived or was this a lie, a tease, a cheat imposed by lifelessness itself?

He glanced at Ramona, *tried to at least*, but a stabbing pain in his neck caught him off guard. What light there was came from a hallway leading out of the room. It was enough to see by, but what he saw near him shocked him cold. Sometime during their encasement in torture, *she* had stopped moving.

Neil groaned as he rolled onto his hands and knees, preparing to crawl to her side. Every muscle and joint screamed its agony. He reached a tentative hand to touch her neck. He felt for the carotid artery and found a pulse. Lightheaded from the release of tension, he sat back, breathing a sigh of relief. There was something he had to attend to. He tried to focus, but his thoughts were slow to return. Two men … two dangerous men … where were they? He looked around for them but they were gone.

Guardedly, he stretched and flexed in every direction to work off the aches and pains, but a little drummer inside his skull hammered with unrelenting stubbornness. The little villain even made seeing straight difficult.

If Ramona awoke in as much pain as he was in, he didn't want her to suffer this cold, hard floor as well. Ignoring the nastiness that permeated every fiber of his being, Neil managed to gather Ramona carefully into his arms, but climbing to his feet proved an exercise in discipline. At last he stood.

In his arms, she awakened, raised her head to see him, then fell limp.

She was a small woman, and ever so light, but he walked stiffly and staggering a bit as though he carried a cow. He took her through the open door, down the hall, and into her bedroom.

After laying her on her bed, Neil paused a moment trying to unscramble the mess in his mind. Puzzled, he looked around. Her room? When did this become her room?

"*Celestria?*"

"Yes, sir?" the ship responded promptly in that familiar soft feminine tone.

"This is the first time I've ever been aboard you, right?"

"Yes, sir."

"That being the case, how is it, then, that I know you better than I know myself? I even know your name."

"You have been prepped, sir."

"Prepped?"

"Prepared, sir. Before you could be allowed full access to me, I needed to genetically alter you."

Neil exhaled, taken aback by what he had just heard. "*Celestria*?" He hesitated, afraid of what the truth might be. "What did you do? Did you 'Prep' Ramona too?"

"I inserted genetic material into your DNA to give you knowledge of me and my functions. Bound together in this way, I now belong to you, and you to each other. This was given you by the Creator." The ship continued. "And yes, sir, this was done to Ramona as well. It was necessary. I am sorry the process was painful."

Neil shook himself. Pain didn't describe half of what he felt, and every distressing answer given by this ship only raised more questions. He wasn't up to spending time he didn't have playing "ask and answer." His situation needed to be assessed and dealt with, and he had to do it through the worst hangover of his life.

"My Lieutenants, where are they?"

"They are in the cavern mounting their ships. They will reposition shortly, and fire upon us. Isn't this what you wanted?"

Neil clenched his teeth but kept his head. Though the question was soft, to Neil it was a clear rebuke.

"How long before they're ready?"

"Five minutes, sir."

"Report! Are you ready and able to fly?"

"Yes, sir."

"Can you get us out of here?"

"Yes, sir."

"Then fire up the drive and head for the surface."

"Yes, Captain." With no more dispute, the ship responded in obedience. Neil was master. Through his feet, he felt the floor faintly thrum as the Slip-band drive came to life.

Ramona roused and, with a moan, sat up on the edge of the bed. He could see she felt the soreness as well, but, thankfully, she had remained unconscious through the worst of the procedure. She stretched and groaned again.

"You okay?" he said.

She looked at him as if his question was glaringly stupid.

"I need to get to the bridge. In moments, my Lieutenants will fire on this ship. Time is critical."

"Sure." Ramona shook her head, puzzled. "And I know *where*, or even *what* the bridge is … how?"

Neil's lips curled into a smile. "I'll help you sort out the *hows* and *whys* later. Right now I need to leave you alone. You okay?"

"I'm right with you."

"Bridge." Neil commanded.

Instantly, a once-smooth wall, like the iris of

a camera, opened to frame a circular portal directly to the bridge. A mix of understanding and seeing something completely new clashed in Neil's mind as genetic memory sought to override his experiences. "Hmm, would you look at that?"

Stepping through, he was on the bridge, half the length of the ship and up three floors in an instant. Grateful that the distance was so greatly reduced, he hobbled stiffly toward the pilot's seat like an old man who had misplaced his walker.

"So," kidded Ramona, "how's this for moving quickly?" As she had said, she was right behind him.

Not knowing she had followed, Neil turned with a start, but a stab in his ribs nailed him hard. He could feel the ship rise slowly as he sat down at the pilot's console. Ramona took the co-pilot's seat next to him. The ship rose to the cavern ceiling and stopped suddenly with a thud. The abrupt jerk sent pain shooting through both of them.

"*Celestria*, we're in enough pain as it is," Neil said. "Please bring inertia suppressor on line."

"Aye, sir."

Thunderous scraping echoed through the bridge as the ice resisted the ship's efforts. Following orders, *Celestria* stubbornly pressed upward and broke through the thick frozen barrier. Once free, the ship began to move more quickly through the softer snow.

Ramona rubbed a temple, scowling at the painful noise filling the bridge. "Buffer that racket, will you, *Celestria*?" At once, the intense sound vanished.

She tabbed the console to bring shields to full. "Give us tactical, *Celestria*."

Just as a 3-D hologram appeared before them revealing the ice planet, Neil shot an annoyed glance her way. "What do you think you're doing?"

"My job." She tabbed her console. The picture zoomed in, and they could now make out the five *Darts* that patrolled the planet's surface. The hologram magnified again, and through the transparent view of Chagwa, they could see their ship deep beneath the snow heading skyward followed by both the Lieutenants' *Dart* fighters.

"Await my commands," Neil ordered. "I'll let you know what to do and when."

Ramona leaned back and glowered. "Excuse me? Who put you in charge?"

Neil fought to clear his mind, and could see Ramona fared no better. "They're closing in. I don't need your mucking about confusing the issue."

Her jaw tightened noticeably as she shook her head. "You just mind what's in front of you and let me do my job." She said motioning to his console.

"I'm in command, woman. Respect that."

"Keep us out of pistol shot, *Celestria*," Ramona ordered, "but don't let them fall too far behind."

"Roger, ma'am," the ship responded.

"Now just one minute here. You'll follow my orders, *Celestria*. Not those of a ... a waitress," he sputtered.

"When Captain French is wrong, sir, I'll disobey those orders. But until then ..."

Ramona grinned. "Like I said, flyboy, who put you in charge? It doesn't sound as if *Celestria* has."

It didn't pay to argue. Time was crucial, and he had none to waste. Seeing Ramona was determined to fight him every step of the way about his being in command, Neil groused to himself, then spoke to regain control. "Back tactical out a bit. Give me a broader picture."

"Yes, Captain."

Ramona rubbed her temples with both hands, trying to ease the soreness, but her actions were in vain. Thinking clearly seemed as much an effort for her as it did for him.

Panning back, the planet's moon came into view. Ramona leaned forward and pointed. "Get us around to the other side of Chagwa's moon, and as soon as we're out of view, go to full stealth."

"Yes, Captain."

"Now, wait a minute, woman. We should head for open space and run like nobody's business."

"What? Why?"

"It's like I said, someone has to be in charge, and I'm the one with the military experience.

"So, it certainly isn't going to be a waitress from Seychelles when it comes to a military operation, huh?"

Neil's mood had instantly soured, but he couldn't tell what aggravated him more, seeing *his* own men trying to kill him, or suffering this young upstart's attitude.

"It's like *Celestria* said, Neil. Correct me when I'm wrong, but until then, mind your own station."

"Yeah, Ramona, walk us right into a trap, will you? I'm not going to let that happen."

"Your men are behind us, Neil," she said coolly. "All of them. How is ducking behind that moon going trap us?"

He sat hunched over his console. "I see that my one good deed in rescuing you has come back to bite my butt. I can't explain my every decision, woman. You'll just have to yield to my experience."

Ramona's voice was quiet but confident. "Neil, let's just get through this. For whatever reason, I know what I'm doing. I can't say why, but I know everything from the ship's name, to understanding what we're up against. Learn to live with this new dichotomy will you?"

Naïve young woman.

Fine.

Live and learn.

Who knows, maybe he was wrong. He shook himself. Blast! He had to stop second guessing himself. He'd calm himself, give her the reins, and correct any mistakes she'd make, then she'd come to learn why his military experience trumped everything else.

Then it dawned on him, naïve or not, she deserved better than what she got on Atheron. He'd muscle past pirates and patrols; past traps and hidden dangers, and everything else thrown at them between here and Providence to get her to safety … and out of his hair. If that, and that alone was to be his one good deed, then so be it. He'd make it happen.

Chapter 9

Compassion

BLOWING white powder a quarter mile into the air, the ship exploded from the frozen snow with both *Darts* in hot pursuit. As the other five interceptors took up the chase, Troy and Jessup headed for the refinery to refuel.

In another moment Neil and Ramona were clear of Chagwa's atmosphere, well on their way to its moon. The *Darts* struggled to keep up as this new ship pressed forward.

"Warning... danger," alerted *Celestria* as she swung the tactical display around to the dark side of the moon.

Neil tensed. As he had guessed, two ships hid in its shadow. "They look like Corsairs."

"Pirates?" Ramona said in surprise. "Who wouldda guessed?"

"They're just waiting for easy pickin's."

Ramona eased back in her chair. "Good."

A throbbing head impaired his ability to think. "We're disadvantaged, waitress. What could possibly be good about having our escape blocked?"

Without taking her eyes from the screen, she smiled with intent. "Neil, haven't you heard? Disadvantage brings to light the more clever captain. *Celestria*, I want the engines to look like they're over-heating."

"Can do, Captain. At your command."

"Reduce speed. Let the *Darts* catch us right

59

when we're in range of the Corsairs."

Catching on to what she wanted, Neil realized she had quickly come up with a good plan. Where did that come from? he thought.

"Get ready to take it from here, Neil."

Neil tabbed his console to ready their plan. To all others it would seem as if their over-heating engines would soon go critical.

"Going to *Level-B stealth* in five seconds."

Neil heard himself boldly say what should have sounded like nonsense, but he understood completely. Through intense pain he and she had learned all about this unique spacecraft in a matter of moments. Lightning fast, technical data now scrolled through Neil's head. The ship had three stealth levels: *Level-A* would make the ship completely undetectable, rendering no readings at all. *Level-B* made the ship appear other than it was by projecting readings such as the over-heated engines.

Unlike any other vessel, *Celestria* could cast a *Sensory Shadow-ship*, a holographic projected craft identical to her in every way—size, shape, color; except the fake ship had no real substance. Combining that feature with *Level-A* stealth mode would leave their adversaries unaware of the true events.

"Creating a *Sensory Shadow-ship*," Neil said, "and going to *Level-A*. I'll drop a class-2 Nuke and give us separation in 5 seconds."

Neil placed the small nuclear bomb where the shadow-ship's engine core should be, had it been the real ship, and then pulled the now invisible ship away. Taking *Celestria's* place, the *Shadow-ship* made it easy for the real ship to sneak away undetected.

Ramona whispered as if her voice would betray their true position. "Looks like they're taking the bait, Neil."

"Aye, Cap. Easing away," Neil responded quietly.

"Careful now."

"As soon as both parties are within gunshot of our shadow-ship. I'll detonate the bomb."

"Good job, Neil. Each party will think the other shot first."

"*Cel*, resume control." Neil said, easing back from the controls. "Get us to a safe distance, and hold position there."

Ramona made little effort to hide her distain. "We could wait and watch these clowns hash out their differences ... or we could simply head to safety. Providence Prime awaits, does it not?"

"Watching the pending butchery makes little sense to you, does it?" Neil kept a close eye on the screen.

"Well, no, actually. I see no reason to stay."

Neil rubbed his neck. "Ramona, go fix yourself some lunch. I'll be down in a bit."

Ramona shook her head and scowled. "Let's leave these fools to their own destruction."

"You don't want to stay? Fine. Go occupy your time with something else. I'm sure this ship is full of distraction."

"Can we just move on?" Ramona said, her tone growing irritable.

"Do what you will. I'm staying put to the end."

"I don't think so."

"Will the wonders never cease? You know, for a fleeting moment back there, I thought you knew what it was to be a captain. Now, by the wildest stretch of my imagination, I simply don't see why I'd think such a silly thing."

"I am a captain," she grumbled. "I just hate having to watch these idiots go at it. Why would you want to stay for the show? Got some morbid need to keep score?"

Ignoring her, Neil tabbed his console. The fake ship exploded in a flash of light that quickly vanished, dissipating into the vacuum of space.

He turned to Ramona. "*Celestria* and I will take it from here, Trog. Why don't you go to the galley and fix yourself something to eat? Maybe a meal will help you get back to feeling less ... Troggish. I'll be down in a bit."

Coldly angry, Ramona conceded. "Galley, please."

The flat wall behind them dilated to form the iris portal. Through it, Neil saw a stainless steel kitchen and almost heard it call her by name. Two steps through the huge iris and the wall closed behind her, smoothing to hide its secret perfectly.

Neil muttered softly to himself, "She's got a heart of stone, that one."

"No, sir. She does not," *Celestria* said in its usual soft, feminine voice. "She's just not a *battle scene* and *carnage* kind of girl, sir."

"Yeah, sure. So what does she think happens to soldiers in space? Chances of survival are slim at best. Zilch if everyone thought as she did."

"She just wasn't thinking, sir."

"Never a truer statement said, *Cel*. I'm just glad to get her off my bridge."

As expected, when the smoke of the explosion cleared, the *Darts* spotted the pirate ships, and vice versa.

Neil could almost sense his former men wanting revenge against the pirates. He, as their commander, had betrayed their trust, and in an instant the pirates had snatched their vengeance from them, or so Neil had made it seem. He imagined the angry thoughts of his men. *We'll have our revenge all right. One way or another we will settle the score.*

The pirates, on the other hand, would have nothing of these soldier boys stealing their prey. Neil had dealt with their kind before, having worked undercover among such men, and he knew, more or less, how they would see things.

Two Corsairs against seven small Darts? Why not? Bring it on! he pictured them boasting. *Maybe we can salvage a Coalition cannon or two, or even an engine core reactor. If nothing else, we can sell the pilots into slavery.* Skilled at survival, pirates were no fools in battle, and Neil's men shouldn't take them lightly.

Well versed in battle tactics, Neil and his

men had learned the pirate's secrets well —sly Lt. Troy Younger the best among them—but despite that, his ship was the first to get hit. Spinning out of control, his *Dart* scattered across 10 acres of the moon's surface.

Knowing he could do nothing to prevent it, Neil felt his chest tighten. Only moments ago, he had stood shoulder to shoulder with the man. Truly, the loss of Troy's life was senseless. Then he remembered *Celestria's* warning, "This may be the last chance to get it right." He felt a chill steal down his back. Troy had made the wrong choice.

The *Darts* swarmed the Corsair that had taken out their chief, ignoring the other one altogether. They hit it hard, and harder still, before turning their attention back to the second ship. Neil approved, but at the same time hoped his men would call off the attack. Except for revenge, there was nothing to be gained.

With no attention paid him by the *Darts*, the second Corsair moved in close to his partner to cover his buddy's vulnerable areas. Even so, the swift and agile *Wolverines* gave the pirates' gunnery a good showing.

As the battle raged, from a safe distance Neil sat in silence watching each of his friends fall in turn. His heart sank.

This would prove to be a costly battle for both sides, leaving no clear winner. After all was said and done, after the last gun had cooled, only one Corsair limped away from this bloody battle. For the heavy price it had paid, it bought only wounds to lick in secret.

The *Wolverines*, on the other hand, now reduced to chunks of metal and bits of debris, wouldn't leave at all; accept for two well-timed escape pods.

Finding his way through the scuffle without being detected was no easy task, but Neil managed somehow to get there and rescue the adrift pods before the pirates could salvage them and enslave the survivors. The pilots Neil had rescued he dealt with first. *Celestria* rendered both men unconscious before having them brought aboard. Although Neil wanted to make himself known to them, he figured doing so was too risky. They had seen *Celestria* explode and to them Neil was dead. Best leave it that way, he thought. If the pilots knew he had survived, *Celestria* was right, he'd be a hunted man.

For the time being, each was given his own small, Spartan room disguised holographicly to look like any prison cell on a pirate ship. This was better than either cramped escape pod, but only just.

Once Neil had time to catch up on his rest, he would look in on both men to see to their needs. But for now he'd have to consider the best way to make his presence known to them, if at all. This was probably the most complicated circumstance he'd ever been in.

The tough job was recovering the bodies of his one-time friends, the men who hadn't survived this clash. Troy's was the only body he couldn't get to, and so he left Chagwa's moon heartsick he couldn't lay to rest his longtime friend.

Distraught that he even let his men die without raising a finger to help, or fight alongside them, he somberly gathered the bodies of *Wolverine* Squad into the cargo bay, tearfully spoke words of regret over each man, and from there, sent them, one at a time, into Chagwa's sun.

Turning to head to the galley, Neil nearly tripped over his helmet. He picked it up. Stupid hash marks had yet to be dealt with.

"*Cel*, I need some white paint and a small brush."

"You'll find those things in the repair shop, sir."

Chapter 10
Building Trust

THE wall irised open to the galley and Neil stepped through from the cargo bay.

Ramona sat at the breakfast bar and slid a plate toward an open seat across from her.

Still feeling stiff, Neil poured himself a drink, eased gingerly into the chair, releasing an uncomfortable breath, then took a bite of the sandwich, half expecting to taste a chemically synthesized over-processed meat-vegetable substitute wedged between two pieces of cardboard like that served by the military. But this … *this* was heaven. He rolled his eyes in ecstasy and swallowed. His appetite suddenly put in an appearance, and Neil consumed half his sandwich in short order. He gestured toward the uneaten half.

"This is great. What is it?"

"Just a little something *Celestria* came up with. It was made to meet your nutritional needs as well as excite your pallet. Go figure."

"My compliments, *Celestria*. You did a wonderful job." He took another bite, rolled his eyes in contentment, and tackled the second half of the sandwich.

"Thank you, Captain Avery," that soft voice said. "Will there be anything else?"

"Nothing more, thank you." He popped the last bite into his mouth, washed it down with his drink, and leaned back.

Ramona eyed him with curiosity. "I see you've come in from the cargo bay instead of from the bridge."

Her pleasant attitude suggested she had forgotten his 'Trog' comment on the bridge. Happy to let it lie, he forced a sly smile.

"Not going to say, hmm? A man with a secret."

His smile fell away.

Yes, he had a secret he'd just as soon keep to himself; the fact that he now regretted his past deeds bothered him considerably. He didn't like being nagged by a ... by a conscience. Burying such emotions, pushing them to the back of his mind was no longer as easy as it once was.

She caught his blank stare, which seemed to make her self-conscious. "What? Do I have spinach in my teeth or something?"

He shook himself from his morose thoughts. "Oh, I was thinking, Miss French, just this morning you were minding your own business waiting tables."

"Mr. Avery, for somebody who wants to be Captain, you can't even keep track of time."

Neil glanced at the ship's chronometer, which now displayed the real reason for his fatigue, *Six A.M.* He had been awake for twenty-six hours straight. "I'm the one who's made space my home. That more than qualifies me to captain *Celestria*. The only question I have is; what am I to do with you?"

She leaned across the breakfast bar and gave

him a stern look. "What are you to do with me? What am I to do with you, Captain Avery, when you still think you're in charge?"

"Oh, are we back to that?"

"I'm not yours to do with as you please. I am a free woman."

"Hmm, so you are."

"And *you* are a free man. How does it feel?"

Was he? Did any of his actions really make him a *free* man? He considered the ache that still wracked his body. Was it recompense for the *Emperor's Princess*? If so, then what was Ramona's pain payment for? Perhaps a bit of sleep would help him figure things out.

"I'm tired. It's been a long day, woman. We have a long trip ahead of us. With all these pirates and patrols about, if we ever return, it's certainly going to be a dangerous haul."

"That's it!" Ramona's sudden outburst nearly jolted Neil out of his chair.

"What? What did I say?"

The woman's eyes brightened, beaming with enthusiasm. "I've been wracking my brain for an appropriate name for this ship. What do you think of *Dangerous Haul*?"

"Excuse me?"

"*Dangerous Haul*. Look, she's stark white with no markings. We can't continue like this can we? We need a disguise, and I was thinking … how about that of an old freighter? We could name it *Dangerous Haul*, right?"

"Can you do that?"

"With your help, sure. You know best what

is least likely to attract attention. Give me a hand with some input, will you?"

The shake of his head was slight, but its meaning should be clear to her. "I'm pretty tired, girl. Maybe tomorrow."

"Neil, have you considered the complexity of this ship?" Ramona turned and looked toward the living room and then turned back to study the galley cabinets, fixtures, and utilities. "She's an unusual, unique spaceship, but there's more to *Celestria* than meets the eye. She belongs to both of us so I believe we ought to work on things like this together."

"Sure, Miss French. Tomorrow?"

"Well yeah, but—"

"Look. She's not a freighter by any stretch of the imagination. She's a yacht."

"A yacht, huh? Then how do you explain that huge cargo bay at her center? Three stories high, eighty feet long of what, exactly?"

Neil shrugged. "Okay. So this yacht has a very …, *very* big … luggage compartment."

Ramona leaned forward, her eyes, cool and determined. "So, what are you saying?"

"Just that getting her to look like an old freighter will take some doing, and I need to crash for a few, catch up on my rest before I tackle a project this big."

"Yeah. Okay."

"Look. While I snooze, you can work up some preliminaries, okay."

Ramona dropped her gaze in disappointment before looking back up. "See you after?"

He gently took her hand. "Or during?"

She snapped her hand back. "Good night, Mr. Avery."

"Trogs," Neil said coldly as he got to his feet. "You people ever have fun?" Without waiting for an answer, he headed to his room.

"WHEN you had the chance, *Celestria*," Ramona asked, "why, didn't you remove his 'Vulgar' gene?"

"Ramona," *Celestria* said, "do you know why he stayed to the end of this last battle?"

"I suppose it was that same stupid gene. Like I said, why didn't you remove it when you had the chance?"

"Neil Avery isn't without his faults, ma'am, but he has a good heart."

"And you derive that farfetched idea from where, exactly?"

"You have two rescued men on board. At great risk to himself, he recovered two life pods, ma'am. That was the real reason he stayed, not because of some gruesome interest in battle. He also wanted to bury his friends; those that didn't make it."

"Oh." Ramona dropped her eyes. "I haven't

given the man much of a chance, have I? Some Christian I've been."

"So, you're not without your faults, either?"

"Apparently not."

"All Captain Avery wants is to discover who you really are. He may be crude at times, but you can trust him to respect your virtue. How did you get to your bed, Capt. French, when you were unconscious?"

Ramona speared fingers through her hair to scratch her head. "He did that?"

"Despite the tremendous pain he was in, he displayed remarkable compassion toward you, someone he thinks he should hate."

"When I think back, in the short time I've known him, he has done nothing but save me, hasn't he? He spared my life when he should have taken it, gotten me off planet at his own expense, and twice put himself between me and a bullet. Why would he do that? And why does he keep calling me 'Trog?'"

There was a moment of silence before *Celestria* answered. "Although he himself doesn't yet know, I'm certain you do."

Celestria had given Neil's memories to Ramona and hers to him. Seeing herself as he had, Ramona envisioned his approaching her at the tavern yesterday morning, and felt the mix of emotions that had flooded his mind. Yes, she knew just how he had felt, and understood what had raged in his heart … although he did not.

But given what she now knew to be true … what should she do with that?

72

Chapter 11

In the Brig

WILLIAM ROBERT TAFT awoke once again in the dank little room. By a dim ceiling luminary he saw dingy walls, a floor seldom mopped, and an iron door blocking his only exit. And the odor … well … a well-worn, never-washed tube sock lost and forgotten in the bottom of Bubba McGirk's gym locker would have smelled as good as a cheeseburger if compared to what now assaulted him. He thought he'd get used to it at some point. No such luck.

He sat up and, after a moment of trying to settle the spasms in his gut, got to his feet. His bed was a sheetless mattress tucked in the corner. A pirate ship must have retrieved his lifepod from the battle scene. Soon he'd be sold into slavery. His head dropped, and that's when he noticed a shock-collar had rubbed his neck raw. By feel, he could tell it was a T-1 Bradshaw, a rather old model used by dog owners to control their pets.

Good. At least that's a plus. Training he thought he'd never use would finally come in handy. Shortly, the collar would be useless.

From outside the room came a metallic clank and what sounded like a jangle of keys. "Back away from the door," came a shout from beyond it.

Taft stepped back. A screech of metal on

metal and the door slid into its wall pocket.

An old man hesitated in the entry. Dressed oddly in clean, bright colors, his garb was a mismatched array of dark leather calf-high boots, a white shirt decorated with frilly lace, a red denim vest, and a black, heavy, high-collared coat trimmed in gold. Had the man a sword dangling on his hip, the pirate costume would have been complete. With tray in hand, he stepped in. "Back away now," he chortled in a friendly voice. "I got yer grub, and if'n you want it you'll back yersef up some."

Billy stepped back and knelt to retake the mattress. "Where am I, old man?"

"Old man?" the codger cackled, "I ain't old by no account. Tain't more'n fifty-five says I, so you jus' mind yersef or I'll set ya straight on that account right quick."

When the pirate stooped to set the tray on the floor in front of the young Enforcer, Billy sprang up, caught the pirate by the collar and slammed him against the wall. "Where am I, old man? How do I get off this ship?"

With one hand, the pirate took hold of Billy's heavy leather dog collar, nearly strangling him with his fat knuckles pressed hard against Billy's Adam's apple. The pirate slowly lifted him from the floor.

Thoroughly amused, the pirate cackled again as Billy's feet dangled midair.

"Son, I'm in charge of this here brig. You behave and take holt o' what I'm sayin,' and you'll save yersef a boatload o' grief. You get me?"

Billy coughed and tried to speak, but the best he could manage was a faint, raspy whisper. "Yes, sir. I get you clear enough."

"That's it? That's the bes' you got in a 'pology?"

Billy was certain his whole head was turning blue. The room was growing dark.

"Sorry ..." he said weakly.

The pirate let him down and shoved him back onto the bare mattress.

Billy coughed, and looked up at the old pirate in disbelief, wondering where so much strength hid in such a feeble frame.

"What are your plans for me?" he managed to croak.

The pirate cocked his head. "Captain says they's a farmer in Providence territory lookin' for good stock. Pay top dollar for the likes of you—young, learnable—not so strong as he wants, but that'll change." He chortled again. "Yes indeed, that will change onest ya start toten hay, that's for sure. Build you up strong, quick, toten hay will."

"Farmer?" Billy frowned. "Not if I can help it!" He pulled himself up on an elbow. "Look. I got money saved back on Parandi. Tell your Captain I'll buy myself from him at twice what that farmer will pay. Just drop me off anywhere this side of the border, and I'll wire the money into any account you want, and say no more."

The pirate snorted. "You talk funny, boy. Wut kind of accent is that anyways?"

"Just tell your Captain, will you?"

"Eat cha grub 'fore I forces it down yer fool throat," the pirate snarled before headed out.

Once in the hallway, with the door closed behind him, the pirate stepped up to Ramona. His holographic camouflage disappeared.

With arms folded, Ramona leaned against the wall.

Neil glanced back at the closed door. "*Celestria*, thanks for the added strength. Your energy beams made me seem stronger than even I could've imagined."

"You're welcome, sir. I was glad to be of assistance."

"So, now what?" Ramona said, turning to head for the galley.

Neil followed at a casual distance. "We drop him somewhere this side of the border. He'll go back and report that everyone was killed by pirates."

"You think he bought it, huh?"

"What? You don't think I'm a convincing buccaneer?"

"Your costume seems pretty silly to me, Neil. Do pirates really wear stuff like that?"

"Flamboyant, garish?"

She turned to face him and shook her head in dismay. "Outlandishly over-the-top?"

"I'd like to think of myself as ostentatious, woman. You betcha pirates dress like that, yes they do. Most pirates want folks to remember them as daring. And there's a certain intimidating air surrounding loud—"

"Clothing?"

"I was going to say … people."

"Yeah, well …" Ramona entered the galley and requested eggs, bacon, and toast for each of them. Then she turned to Neil. "Do you think gruel is all we should serve our guests?"

Neil went to the fluid dispenser to order coffee for Ramona and himself. "Only Billy Taft. The boy seems to have his heart set on returning to the Coalition."

"And Carlton?"

Neil took a seat at the breakfast counter. "Nah, he seems pretty docile. When I told him he'd be working a farm, the kid almost lit up. I believe he's glad to be shed of the Coalition and life as an Enforcer."

"You think downing the cruise liner took the fight out of him?" Ramona slid his hot breakfast plate to Neil.

"Carlton is a good kid, but there's still a chance he's just playing us, waiting for a good time to strike. *Celestria*, any opinion on Carl?"

"I've been monitoring his vital signs, Captain, and I believe he's genuine."

"We can trust him, huh?" Ramona said. "Enough to give him access to you, *Cel*?"

"Capt. French, you and Capt. Avery can decide that for yourselves, but I would give it much consideration before going that far."

Neil and Ramona finished their breakfast in silence, each debating the prospect within themselves. Neil stood, gathered the plates, and took them to the sink.

Ramona's bemused expression cradled disbelief. "Going to do them by hand?"

As Neil ran water over them, he gave her a quick look. "Helps me think. I'm not sure what to do with Carl just yet. We should take him on to Providence, but whether we fake his escape or just let him go, I haven't decided."

"We could add him to our crew."

Neal didn't like the idea of adding Carl to their troubles, but held his tongue. Carl would only complicate the tenuous state of affairs already on board. A plan was formulating in Neil's mind that involved neither Carl nor Ramona, a plan that would impact everyone but would have consequences deadly only to himself.

He turned off the water, dripped in *Celestria's* homemade dish-soap, and slowly ran the scrub brush over a plate.

"Neil?" Ramona said. "We could add Carl to our crew."

"I heard you …" He looked up but hesitated. "… but I don't know what to tell you, Ramona. Things are happening so fast I haven't had time to screw my head on straight. Can I think about it?"

Chapter 12

A New Look

AFTER getting "*the animals*" fed, and breakfast dealt with, Neil spent a few hours tackling navigation and other issues before heading to the cargo bay. The soreness, though not totally gone, had been reduced to tolerable levels. Before a jog around the bay, he took time to flex and stretch raw nerves and tender muscles, stooping to start with those his legs, then moved on to those in his back, neck, and arms.

Ramona entered the bay from the iris door wearing a tank top, runner's shorts, track shoes, and a satisfied expression. Suspiciously, her disposition had changed since breakfast.

She carried something—a bundle of ...

"Before we change *Celestria's* outward appearance, Neil," she said. "I'd like to change yours. That flight suit has got to go." She handed him the bundle, track shoes wrapped in a man's jogging shirt and shorts.

"Thank you, Ramona. This is great. I'll be right back."

"No, no. You can change right here."

"What?"

"*Celestria?*" A bench appeared. As if to watch Neil change, Ramona took a seat. "Well, don't be shy, go ahead."

Dumbfounded, he looked at the outfit, and then back at her. "I really don't think—"

"No, really. Go ahead."

He looked at her in dismay, then said, "Fine. Enjoy." Tossing the shoes and shirt to the bench beside Ramona, he stripped from his suit and pulled the shorts over his briefs.

Wearing a coy smile, Ramona didn't turn away.

When he grabbed the shirt from the bench, he realized something was up. Ramona didn't seem to see him. He glanced back only to see a holographic him standing there wearing a stupid grin.

"Oh, cute," he said as he tugged the shirt over his head. "Real peachy, girlfriend."

As he took a seat next to Ramona to pull on his socks and shoes, the holographic him disappeared.

Ramona turned to him. "Nervous were you?"

"Decided to let me twist, huh? No, no. I get it. You and *Celestria* were just having fun."

"Not really. *Cel* veiled you in invisibility, and created a *Shadow you* to entertain me while you changed. What was funny was the goofy expressions your Holo-you made behind your back. *Cel* did her best to make me laugh, but I held it together. I did a good job, don't you think?"

"Yeah … wonderful." Neil jumped to his feet and started around the bay's perimeter.

In another moment Ramona passed him, giggling like a schoolgirl as she went.

Try as he might, he just couldn't catch up to

her, eventually having to stop to catch his breath. Ramona ran three more circuits before stopping by his side—not breathing hard at all.

"Are you trying to make a point, Miss?"

"I jogged every day before work, flyboy. Hit the showers, and I'll make lunch."

Neil showered and found new clothes laid out on his bed.

After lunch, Ramona nodded toward the living area. "Care to relax while we discuss *Celestria's* new look?"

They were surprised to find there, suspended in the middle of the room, a ten-foot holographic replica of *Celestria*. It was, just as Ramona had said, stark white, but at both its bow and stern was the name, *Dangerous Haul*.

Ramona settled into a well-cushioned chair. Seeing the hologram and the immeasurable possibilities to play seemed to give her energy.

Neil felt his every muscle relax as he nestled into the other cushy, leather-like sofa.

"All right, *Celestria,*" Ramona said, "I'm ready. Let's see you in a checkerboard motif."

Instantly, the white ship sported black and red squares from nose to tail.

Ramona's eyebrows rose nearly to her hairline. "Impressive," she breathed, and then she got down to serious playtime. "How about a Currilian racing sloop."

The red and black squares vanished to be replaced with an overall forest green, stripes of red and gold intersected at right angles at the ship's prow. Garish was the only word for that pattern. For the next half hour Ramona changed *Celestria's* appearance with what Neil thought was every variation of color, pattern, and style possible. Making no comment, he let her work, knowing instinctively that this was more than play. It was necessary training.

Without effort his thoughts drifted from the task to the woman herself. Although her focus was intense, her delicate features captivated his attention. The gleam in her eyes that spelled a playful mischievous nature hid well her ornery streak. Oh, yeah, he'd already experienced that! But still, she was a mystery nonetheless.

The way she looked at designing this ship's cover was almost childlike in its purity, yet deep inside those dark eyes sat a compelling wisdom comfortably enthroned in good cheer. As she played, she seemed young but also very mature. Perhaps there was more to her than Neil had first suspected, perhaps not; … maybe it was only a full belly and the attention of a pretty girl getting the better of him.

When Ramona glanced his way, Neil suddenly realized he'd been staring. Snapped back to reality, he turned quickly to the hologram, but not fast enough. Mesmerized by her smile, he was slow to keep his fascination secret. He grimaced, and from the corner of his eye saw her cock her head to study *him*—but, instead, she spoke to the ship.

"Okay, time to get serious. Let's see how you look dark gray." Instantly the holographic ship changed color. "Now give us a yellow band from bow to stern," Ramona added, and instantly the yellow band appeared.

"Underscore that with a thinner bright red band," Neil said, and it, too, appeared.

"Looking good, Neil. But still …"

He nodded. "It looks a little too sharp, wouldn't you say?"

"Uh huh. You're pretty perceptive."

His attention was drawn more toward her than to the ship. To hold his interest at bay, Neil gulped loudly … *too* blasted loud, he thought.

"*Celestria*," he said to draw attention away from his embarrassment, "age this model, say … fifteen years, maybe."

The ship's finish dulled a bit, but not enough to suit either person.

"Uh uh," Ramona said, "Not enough. I want *Dangerous Haul* to look as though it were ill kept and poorly piloted. You know, *Celestria*? Like you've had paint scraped off here and there, from moorings and the like."

"Perhaps like this?" *Celestria* said. The hologram changed, and the ship now looked well weathered. Its name, *Dangerous Haul*, could scarcely be made out.

Ramona beamed. "Now we're getting somewhere, but we haven't arrived yet. What are those engines, Neil … that scorch areas of the hull?"

"Ion converters? The exhaust ports do leave a pretty nasty black buildup. They're an antiquated propulsion system, though."

"Yes, that's what I want."

"You're good at this, Ramona. That would be the right look for this ship." He got to his feet and pointed to the areas on both sides behind amidships, just above the *Slip-Band drive*. "*Celestria*, create an Ion engine bulge here, and here, and put believable exhaust ports behind each. And then scorch the ship from the ports on back, like exhaust has built up over the last 15 years."

Ramona walked around the hologram of *Dangerous Haul*. From every angle, it looked like an old freighter that had seen better days. It neither looked like a threat, nor a prize, nor would it draw attention to itself as it crossed the Providence border.

"I think it's good," Ramona finally said.

Neil searched the hologram for any indicator that would alert the border patrol. He had made that run all too often and could spot a smuggler from a good distance. This ship looked like nothing of the sort. "Yes, it does look innocent enough."

"And *Dangerous Haul* fits as a name."

"I believe you're right. *Dangerous Haul* sounds good to me."

"It's decided then?"

Content, Neil shrugged and nodded in approval.

"*Celestria*," Ramona said. "We'll name this persona *Dangerous Haul.*"

"In this guise, Capt. French, I will respond to *Dangerous Haul* as so ordered."

"And you will respond to '*DH*' for expedience' sake as well," Neil added.

"Yes, Capt. Avery. As so ordered."

"One more thing, *Cel*. When you're in this disguise, you'll address Ramona and I as Captain and Mrs. Star. That will be our guise."

"Excuse me?" said a rather perturbed Ramona. "That will be Captain and *Mr.* Star, if you please."

"Perhaps," said *Celestria*. "I should call each of you Captain Star."

Ramona glared at Neil daring him to argue the point.

"Very good, *Celestria*. When you wear this disguise, we'll be Captains Star." Ramona reached out to shake Neil's hand and, though the contact was brief and innocent, all his troubles seem to evaporate at her touch.

Man, he thought, do we make a good team or what? His thoughts stuttered to a stop. What am I thinking? She and I? Yeah, right. Like that could ever happen. We might make good partners for the ship ... for the time being ... but how long can *that* last?

When they reached their destination things would change, probably forever. That seemed the fate cut out for them anyway. As long as

Atheron … as long as the *Emperor's Princess* stood between them, Neil would never get the girl … not that he wanted this particular girl anyway. She's opinionated, has no understanding of authority, and never shuts up. To top all that, she talks with someone she can't even see. How nutty is that?

But then again, she had a really sweet smile … when she wasn't frowning at him.

Enough Neil, he said to himself, put it away and get back to business. He turned from the hologram to her. "Okay, if we're ready, let's get on to Providence then."

Ramona nodded, then turned to him. "Race you to the bridge."

"Sure."

"Winner captains from here on out." Before he could move, Ramona bolted out the door.

"Uh, huh." Neil smirked. Disadvantaged, he called for the iris, and stepped through.

One day, he promised himself, he'd play fair.

He took a seat and swiveled toward the stairs just as Ramona trundled in.

With her hands on her hips, she scowled. "You cheated."

He raised an eyebrow as if her accusation was silly. "Haven't you heard? 'Disadvantage brings to light the more clever captain.' It looks like you'll have to settle for the office of first mate. I understand there's an opening."

She scowled even more. "I demand a rematch, Mister."

Chapter 13
Getting Involved

WITH the core planets left far behind, Neil and Ramona skirted the Dalvus Nebula, a major obstacle to get around.

This morning Neil sat at the helm studying the scanner, or trying to, anyway. He wanted to get Ramona off his mind by focusing on other things, but when she joined him, she ignored the co-pilot's seat, insisting on seeing *his* scanner by leaning over his shoulder. This made his ability to focus … unattainable.

Didn't she realize that her long, soft curls caressed his cheek, or that her fresh, just bathed scent drew his attention closer?

Or maybe she was well aware.

He inhaled deeply to enjoy the moment, then mentally shook himself and spoke to break the spell that was rapidly overcoming him.

He tapped the screen. "If we cut through here, through the Straits of Andus we could shave weeks of travel time from our schedule."

Ramona eased back. "Dangerous move isn't it? Don't pirates control the Straits?"

"Taking the long way around will extend our trip, but it's safer by far."

"Okay, then—"

"Wait a minute." Neil leaned forward and zoomed in on an area directly ahead. "Long-range scanners are picking up something."

Ramona slid into the other chair.

"Looks like a Brigantine and Corsair are chasing a small yacht, Ramona." Neil turned to face her. "The pursuers are closing to gun range and will catch the yacht soon."

"No time to lose, Neil. Guns or helm?"

"Take the helm," he said, transferring control to her. "*Celestria*, we need to get a message to that yacht and not alert the pirates chasing him. How do we do that?"

"I suggest a narrow communication beam directed at the yacht's scanner."

"Yes, do it. Get his attention; tell him to come to heading 29-16, and we'll help."

"And tell them," Ramona added, "*Do not* reply to this message."

With that, the small ship altered course toward *Celestria*.

"I'm loading the rack with class 1 rockets," Neil said, "and targeting the Brigantine."

"Sir," responded *Celestria*, "class 1's will not penetrate the Brigantine's shields."

"That's the idea, *Cel*. Watch and learn."

"Aye, sir."

"Apply '*Prize*' color scheme," Ramona said.

"Aye, Captain French, *Prize* it is."

Neil's favorite color scheme, that of a large, luxurious yacht, was the perfect pirate lure.

As *Celestria* came at the other three ships head-on, Neil armed three rockets. Launching them in succession, the rockets shot ahead of *Celestria*, veered up and over the yacht, passed the Corsair, and one after the other lit up the bow shields of the Brigantine.

"Sir, we are being hailed."

Neil cocked his head. "By whom?"

"The Brigantine *Val Hilliard*, sir."

He glanced up as though the ceiling were the source of his ship's voice, but caught himself. That annoying habit would take effort to break.

"*Celestria*," he said, "create internal persona '*Neil-Ramona 3*,' please."

"Aye, sir."

He glanced at Ramona. "Remember, we want to appear incredibly arrogant, right?"

Sober and focused, she nodded her approval.

He launched three more rockets. "Okay *Celestria*, open communications."

On the big screen, the Brigantine Captain appeared. He was a tall, well-tanned man in a uniform of a sort. "*Prize*, I am Capt. Andrews of *Val Hilliard*. This is not your affair. Please stand down." Right then the three rockets connected with *Val Hilliard*, rattling it a bit. Andrews grimaced and set his jaw.

If the holo-image '*Neil-Ramona 3*' worked correctly, from *Val Hilliard's* bridge Andrews would see Neil and Ramona relaxing in a posh living area. Ramona wore a beautiful Etherian-silk evening dress while Neil was dressed in a fine Sharminia suit. In this guise, they looked well heeled.

With his nose held just a little higher, Neil acted as though he and she were above it all.

Arrogance personified, he spoke as if his every word was glaringly important. "I am Headley Farnsworth, sir, of the Parandine Farnsworths. Capt. Andrews, I must tell you that I will not have you harassing fellow yachtsmen; I simply will not have it. Now heave to immediately or suffer another volley of my best."

Although Captain Andrews' tone was firm and measured, tempered with civility, his brow was knit with amused dismay. "Mr. Farnsworth, this does not concern you. If I were a pirate, I would prefer your craft to the one I pursue, would I not? Now please stand down."

Neil turned and spoke as if to someone off-screen. "Captain, it seems this man will not listen to reason. Close communications." With that the screen went black. *Celestria* shot past the two pursuit ships and turned to follow them.

"Well ... that was different," Ramona said.

"Hmm, that's an understatement." Neil hunched over his screen to make sense of what he saw. "Not pirates, then what's their game?"

"What says they're not pirates, Neil? Even if it's not apparent, to them that little yacht carries something far more valuable than *Prize*."

Neil drew a firm hand down his face. Trying to understand this confusing mess wasn't going to be easy. "Our first instinct was to take the side of the smaller craft. Do you think we may have been wrong in that?"

Deep in thought, Ramona didn't reply.

"Let's try something else." Neil turned back

to his console. "*Celestria*, open a channel to the yacht."

The screen came to life. On it, with a face thick with sweat, a trembling, pudgy, but well dressed man screamed into the monitor. "Help me! They're going to kill me!"

Neil scowled. "My good man, what do these brigands want with you?"

"What? Are you deaf?" he shouted. "They want to kill me."

"Yes, yes," Neil said, still playing the part of a unruffled aristocrat, "but *why* do they want to kill you?"

"I am the Governor of Praxis, and they are instigating a coup." His eyes darted as if frantic for an idea. "Help me elude them, and I'll pay you 25 denalli."

"Humph! More money indeed." Neil said. "I suppose to a few that pittance would seem like a small fortune. But I find your presumption that I lack for money insulting." He turned away. "Close the connection."

"Something's not right," Ramona said. "I can't say why, but I don't trust that man."

Neil glanced at her. "Andrews seems no better. What say we not involve ourselves?"

Celestria sounded an alarm. "Warning, danger! Ambush ahead: two Galleasses, one Xebec, and three Corsairs, all lying in wait."

Ramona spun toward Neil. "Now what?"

Before Neil could think, *Celestria* answered Ramona. "The yacht's pilot knows the other ships are there, ma'am. The yacht turned toward them as if this was his original and intended course heading."

"Looks like a side has been chosen for us," Neil said. "*Cel*, raise *Val Hilliard*."

Andrews appeared on the screen. "I'm rather busy, Mr. Farnsworth. What do you want?"

"Captain, it's a trap." Neil said with an urgency that surprised even himself. "In the nebula dead ahead are two Galleasses."

Andrews' eyes flared in surprise. "How do you know that, Farnsworth?"

"Long-range scanners, sir. You should see them on yours any second now."

Capt. Andrews looked away to study something off screen, nodded to someone, then turned back to Farnsworth.

"All right, ship's signatures are detected. But how do you know *exactly* what they are, *unless* you, sir, are a party to them?"

"My good man, I assure you, my scanners are the latest our technology has to offer. Now tell me truthfully, what's that yacht to you?"

Andrews' square jaw tensed visibly. "I have little reason to trust you, Farnsworth."

Neil threw his hands up in surrender. "Fine, take 'em on by yourselves. This isn't my fight after all, Andrews. Once you're enslaved and your ships are picked clean by space vultures ask yourself if, against those ships, you could've used another gun. If nothing else, sir, *Prize* could've served as bait."

"Bait, huh? Bait for whom: them or me?" Hesitant, Andrews leaned forward as if to dissect Farnsworth's true intentions. "Okay, Farnsworth, it seems I have little choice."

"That would seem to be the case, Capt. Andrews. What's going on?"

Gathering his thoughts, Andrews leaned back. "Governor Chact is aboard that yacht. He taxed us well beyond his government's needs, then embezzled the money and ran. Without his return, Praxis is bankrupt. Our aim, Capt. Boyd of *Star Sword* and I, is to restore what he took and bring him to justice."

In affirmation, Neil nodded. "Understood, Captain. After you reclaim him, head home with all due speed. You'll have two Galleasses and a Xebec hot on your tail."

Andrews' expression changed to one of startled puzzlement. "What—"

Neil closed the channel and turned to Ramona. "Shall we, *Luv*?" he said with a voice dripping with arrogance.

"Let's," she said, increasing speed, passing both ships to catch the small yacht.

Full throttle, six ships shot from the nebula to ambush *Val Hilliard*, *Star Sword*, and *Prize*.

Neil locked a gun onto the yacht and fired. Instantly, the little ship lost all power and dropped to sub-light speed. As *Prize* flew passed it, Neil aimed at the lead Corsair and fired all guns at once, then loaded class three rockets.

Andrews' Brigantine scooped up the yacht and turned back toward Praxis. *Star Sword* followed *Prize* to assist.

The two Galleasses and Xebec ran after Andrews' ship, and as they passed *Prize*, Neil fired a spread of rockets at each ship, to severely damage their shields. *Star Sword* fired all guns at the Xebec to wreck its shields further, and then turned hard and fired again as it passed.

The Galleasses raced on ahead as the crippled Xebec dropped to sub light.

Unable to catch the Galleasses, *Star Sword*, turned to the other Corsairs.

Prize had one smoking, which limped away. The other two Corsairs pounded *Prize* hard before *Star Sword* reached them to fire a torrent of plasma cannon. This drew the enemy ships away from *Prize*, but otherwise did little damage.

Neil launched a swell of rockets to take out one Corsair's sensor array and shields.

It moved off.

The remaining pirate traded hits with the smaller *Star Sword* until both began to jet smoke.

Ramona brought *Prize* closer. With rockets and cannon, Neil hammered the pirate until it broke off its attack, but not in time; *Star Sword* was badly hurt.

Neil opened communications.

In a smoke filled bridge, slumped in *Star Sword's* command chair, a uniformed woman motioned with a feeble hand. "Go. Help Andrews. His Brigantine doesn't have a chance against those Galleasses." She coughed from the smoke.

"Warning!" *Celestria* said.

The blip on the scanner troubled Ramona. "I see it." Although wounded, the returning Xebec still posed a huge problem.

"First things first, Captain Boyd. We've got company coming, and our sensors indicate your ship can't hold together much longer. Launch all of your escape pods ASAP, and we'll return for them after we've taken care of this pressing business."

"Roger, *Prize*," said Boyd before the screen went black. Within minutes, escape pods jettisoned from Star Sword to rocket away to safety.

Ramona eased *Prize* away to engage the Slip-band drive, but the ship shuttered and failed to jump to light speed.

"Warning. Slipdrive is offline. Sub-light thrusters are functioning at ninety percent."

"*Celestria*, what can you give me? We need speed, and we need it now."

"Effecting repairs, Captain French. One moment please." *Cel* picked up speed, but was sluggish and struggled in the effort.

Ahead, the Xebec accelerated toward them, but hadn't yet jumped to lightspeed. Neil ordered *Celestria* to ready all weapons, and then, in warning, turned to his partner.

"Ramona, Xebecs are a pirate's dream ship—"

"It is a heavily armed, extremely fast predator ship," Ramona cut him off, "that once having locked onto its prey can scarcely be shaken. Xebecs have been known to ring the death knell for ships as large as Coalition Destroyers, and, even while wounded, they are quite formidable. This one no doubt returns to focus on *Star Sword*." Keeping her eyes on the console she mechanically rattled off the information without skipping a beat.

Neil's eyebrows practically touched his hairline. "Okaaay, this genetic memory thing still takes some getting used too."

Ramona looked his way. "It's realistic to believe that a man out for revenge captains this Xebec. *Star Sword's* escape pods are at risk. If we can't severely disable the renegade, we'll have to destroy it."

Hearing the note of regret in her voice, Neil saw distress and sorrow mingled with resolve written in Ramona's face.

"There's no other way, Captain."

"No, there isn't."

Neil studied the events on his screen. "*Celestria*, get that engine on line NOW."

"Aye, sir. One moment please."

"You have a plan, Ramona?"

"One's formulating."

"I've got nothing, girl. We better—"

"Got it!" she snapped. All business now, her actions were decisive and steady. "Yeah. Ready the weapons." But when she punched in the command to create a *Sensory shadow-ship*, nothing happened.

"Sorry, Captain French," *Celestria* said. "That feature is currently offline."

As *Celestria's* auto-mend systems continued with repairs, the ship slowly picked up speed.

The Xebec, still a great distance from them, picked up momentum as well, but still hadn't made the jump to light. The first ship to do so would hold the advantage over the other. Against the Xebec's numerous guns, speed would be *Celestria's* only plus.

Neil studied the power indicators and made a mental note of the Xebec's position. "*Celestria*, give me rockets, and load the torpedo chambers."

"Aye, sir."

Ramona seemed stressed. "*Celestria*, are you close to finishing repairs? We have a need for speed, girl. Give us something, will ya?"

In that instant, the ship lurched and jumped to light speed.

Ramona, at the helm, quickly formed a Shadow-ship, but got nothing but a red, flashing, *offline* light for her troubles. The damaged Slipband drive, even when pressed, gave her little better than light speed.

"Come on, girl," Ramona said. "Give me one fold, one lousy little fold, *please*."

Suddenly the ship jumped one-fold to double their velocity.

"Yes! Atta girl!" Ramona patted her console in appreciation, then turned to Neil. "You've got to hit the Xebec before it hits us, Neil. *Celestria* can't take much more pounding."

Hitting the Xebec without killing it could spell certain doom. Because of *Celestria's* alterations, Ramona was as aware of the danger as he.

As they went in, Ramona had to swing *Celestria* wildly to evade the Xebec's guns and get in close enough to make each of her own shots count. Even so, Neil still had to lock on to vital areas just to hurt the big, heavily armored ship. He could run out everything he had along the Xebec's hindquarter and, if not careful, do little more than make it mad.

Neil glared and growled without saying a word. He had faced one of these beasts before but hadn't fared as well as he wanted. In his previous encounter, the Xebec's plating, a celamic-tricoen alloy, exceptional in its ability to transfer zithion energy, had spread the charge over a larger area to lessen the blow. The result; Neil and his men had barely escaped with their lives.

Neil growled again. "This time around, let's see how well you handle rockets, punk."

Time was critical, and the Xebec was the linchpin. Andrews' ship would be lost to the Galleasses if too much time was spent on the Xebec. But if hurrying caused Neil to fail in disabling the beast, those in Boyd's life pods would be at risk of enslavement.

The huge Xebec began to lay down heavy fire as *Celestria* headed in. As she shot past it, one errant shot caught her flank to spin *Celestria* out of control. Ramona fought to regain command as *Cel* swung around hard, only to come to rest behind the Xebec.

As the huge ship started its turn to bring its guns to bear, Neil spotted its one weakness—*every ship had one*—a choice target called the *sweet spot*. For the Xebec, *this Xebec*, it was a vent below and behind its bridge. Neil fired off three rockets in succession, and the bright explosion, near enough to shake *Celestria*, downed the shield and hit the vent.

Before the Xebec could retaliate, Neil fired another round, which tore away the Xebec's conning tower in a blaze of twisted metal.

"Now let's see how well you pilot that bucket of bolts without a bridge, buddy boy."

Ramona pulled hard about and headed for Andrews' ship. "Good shooting, Neil. One down. Now for the Galleasses. *Celestria*, report!"

"I have minor damage throughout my frame and though drive output is down twenty-five percent, I am effecting repairs. The life pods are now safely away from the *Star Sword*."

"Give me tactical," Ramona said.

The 3-D hologram came up to show that the Galleasses had gained on Andrews' ship. *Celestria* was far behind. "How long before the pirates catch *Val Hilliard*?"

"15 minutes." *Celestria* said.

"And what's our ETA?"

"At present, 22 minutes, Captain French."

"Calculate *Val Hilliard's* least survival time."

"Roger, Captain. Three minutes, if the two Galleasses use full fire power."

"We're going to be too late."

Neil swung around to face her. "No, we're not. We've got more time than that. The pirates want to get paid, and their paycheck is aboard *Val Hilliard*."

"Roger that, Neil. Level-A Stealth, please, so they don't detect our approach."

"Negative, Captain. We *do* want them to see us. We need to draw fire away from *Val Hilliard* to give him breathing room."

Uneasy, Ramona shifted in her seat. Her dependence on Stealth was understandable, but this wasn't the time to use it.

"Ramona, I know *Celestria* can't take many more blows, but if we're to give Andrews a fighting chance, we must separate those ships. Stealth mode uses too much energy, which only leaves me with rockets. If those Galleasses have *ARCMs*, then rockets will be useless."

A long sigh spoke of Ramona's reluctance. "All right. If we're going in fully visible, Neil, we'll need to do some fancy flying. Want to take the helm?"

"If you can handle the guns, sure."

At Ramona's nod Neil tabbed his console to transfer the gunnery display to her control and the helm to his.

As they neared the Galleasses sensor range, difficult decisions made Ramona grip her console hard. "Neil, *Prize*, at 180 feet, will hardly be seen as much of a threat. Only half the size of a Corsair and a third the size of a mammoth Galleass ... well ..."

"I see. If both ships ignore us and focus their guns on Andrews, they could convince him to give up his precious cargo."

"That won't do at all," Ramona said. "Gov. Chact is all that's keeping them alive. To give him up would mean enslavement ... or *death* ... for the crew of *Val Hilliard*."

Neil stared at his scanner for a second. Then a sly grin curled his lips. "Since they can't see us at this distance, *Celestria*, cloak yourself with the Xebec's energy readings; *Level-B* Stealth, please. And make this bridge match the Xebec's when com-lines are open."

"Roger, Captain Avery."

Ramona shot a startled scowl at Neil. "I don't see where you're going with this."

"While you're at it, *Cel,* turn Ramona into Capt. Boyd's double."

"What? Uh, uh. *No way.*" Ramona said.

"You can pull this off. I just hope Andrews doesn't blow your cover."

"Well, I'll try, but you better have a plan B." Ramona took a deep breath, and closed her eyes to mentally get into character. "Okay *Celestria*, when we're in *Val Hilliard's* sensor range, open a com-line. And I do mean *wide open* so the pirates and all can listen."

"Roger, Captain French. Coming into sensor range in T-minus 30 seconds." The next moment, *Celestria* hailed *Val Hilliard* and the screen lit up with the image of Capt. Andrews.

Andrews' calm expression covered a mix of hope, relief, and frustration, but didn't hide the surprise in his voice. "Captain Boyd, you've captured the Xebec?"

"Roger, Cap. I'm sorry for the delay, but the Xebec's crew did resist her capture."

Andrews thought quickly, pulled his watch from his pocket, glanced at it, and raised an eyebrow toward the image of Boyd.

"Yes, sir," she said as though reading his mind, "I got cocky and allowed them to put up a fight. But sir, I shall not be so lax with these Galleasses. Or did you wish to take these two apart yourself?"

Andrews glanced again at his pocket watch, and then looked at her sternly. "I have enough notches on my belt, Captain Boyd. This is your chance to build your reputation, so have at them. There are only *two*, so I'll give you five minutes to take them down. And Captain …"

"Yes, sir?"

"… prisoners, please. Dead men make lousy slaves."

Ramona let her lips form a sinister grin.

"Aye, Captain Andrews. Boyd out." With that, the screen went black.

"Well played, Ramona!" Neil was warm and positive. "Andrews caught on quickly, too … for an amateur. Now let's see if it worked."

She sat erect, in her chair. Her fingers, tapping a nervous rhythm on the armrest, were the only sign of the tension she bore.

"Somebody *do* something!" she said.

"Hey! Hey!" Neil cheered. "We're getting a response. One Galleass is cutting and heading for high ground."

"Really?" Ramona sounded like a child who had just aced a test she had no time to study for.

Neil chuckled at the surprised glee lighting her face. Despite the apparent danger, she clearly enjoyed the excitement. As Neil's smile grew he carefully considered her enthusiasm. "Now tell me you weren't great."

Wide-eyed, Ramona couldn't hide her grin, nor did she try. "I was awesome!"

Celestria's soft voice filled the bridge. "We are being hailed by Capt. Andrews."

Ramona squared her shoulders. "Open the com."

With a stern expression, Captain Andrews appeared on the screen. "Change of plans, Captain Boyd. Go after the runner, and I'll use the device on this straggler myself," he said, having guessed the deceptive game Boyd was playing; inventing a mysterious weapon himself.

"Captain Andrews, you're spoiling my fun. I

was looking forward to my first triple capture, but by your command, sir. Boyd out." With that the screen again went black.

Val Hilliard slowed to a stop and turned on its pursuer.

Finding itself now alone and sandwiched between two menacing ships, the remaining Galleass panicked and frantically veered to speed off in a different direction.

Once the Galleass was beyond scanner range, Neil dropped the Xebec's energy readings. Andrews brought his ship back to *Prize*, and together the two returned to *Star Sword*, Boyd, and her crew. Nothing was left but the life-pods and metal debris.

"Looks like vultures will feast tonight, Ramona. I'm just glad it won't be on us."

"I've met my share of Salvage Jacks at the tavern, Neil. Unlike pirates, they're nice people, hardworking, decent folk, really. They're just looking to clean up space debris, especially if they can make a profit from what they salvage."

Prize turned toward Praxis to escort the brigantine back to its home. Along the way, Neil and Ramona couldn't help but notice the deafening silence. Andrews made no gesture of gratitude whatsoever, not that doing so was required, but considering all they'd just gone through … it was a bit odd.

As Praxis came into view, and at seeing no other trap to contend with, Neil and Ramona turned *Celestria* back toward Providence.

"We're being hailed," *Celestria* said.

"Do you think we'll get that *thank you* after all?" Neil said.

"Somehow I doubt it, Neil. *Cel*, open the com, please."

Captains Andrews and Boyd came on the screen. "Mr. Farnsworth, that's some ship you have there. *Prize* is a remarkable craft."

"Not really, Captain. Prize is just a common boat with high dollar tech. You can get similar upgrades for your ship on Parandi."

"We could use a Captain and crew of your abilities," Andrews added, "to help us bring Praxis back on the right path."

Neil forced a polite smile. "What do you expect of me and my ship, Captain? Your government's corrupt. Take care of that, and things will change."

Andrews winced. Apparently Neil's words, catching him off guard, struck a raw nerve. "We could simply seize your ship, Farnsworth. As I see it, the necessities of a whole planet outweigh your individual needs a thousand times over."

"I think that's an absurd argument for thievery, Captain, which makes my point. You need to change your own thinking about such matters before anything else." The screen went black. *Celestria* increased to half sub-light.

The ship jolted. "Sir, they've fired on us," *Celestria* said.

Neil brought *Prize* to a complete stop and turned to the screen in expectation. "You know what, Ramona? I'm thinking Praxis might be a good place to stop for the night."

"Really? I'm not certain that's such a bright idea."

"Trust me. You'll see."

"We are being hailed, sir," alerted *Cel.*

"Put'em on."

When the screen came up, Neil sighed in clear disappointment. "Is this how you repay a kindness, Andrews; with treachery instead of a thank you? So you're a pirate after all, are you?"

Andrews' face was pinched in a harsh scowl. "You will alter course to Praxis, *Trog.* I've stated my case, and I will not debate it with the likes of you." The com-line closed.

Neil scoffed. "Common." Did Andrews really believe hanging *that* label on Neil would get him *Prize*? It was ironic, though, calling Neil a Trog.

With *Val Hilliard* closing behind him, more ships came up from the surface to encircle *Prize* and escort her in; but *Prize* increasingly faded.

Val Hilliard fired a shot, which passed unhindered through the vanishing ghost only to clip the lead escort.

Leaving Andrews with nothing but what he had initially come for—*Gov Chact and the stolen funds*—the invisible *Celestria* headed down to Praxis' surface to implement Neil's next plan.

Chapter 14

The Unexpected

THE now invisible *Celestria* settled into a remote wooded grove on Praxis. Neil switched to *Level B* stealth mode, changing the ship's color to match the foliage, then followed Ramona to the ship's lounge, where she pulled her Bible from a drawer and, with great tenderness, ran her fingers across its face before setting it on the coffee table.

"*Celestria*," Neil said. "Print a copy of this book for me, will ya? I'd like to see why that idiot thought I was a Trog."

"Right away, sir," the ship answered.

"The nerve of that guy, huh, Neil," Ramona said sarcastically.

"Well, yeah. What could I have done to get Andrews to think I was a—"

"Don't you dare!" Ramona snapped.

"A Christian. I was going to say Christian."

Ramona turned to pour each of them a glass of water. "Maybe it had something to do with our self-sacrifice, our sense of justice ..."

"Or our butting in without being asked," Neil teased.

Ramona giggled. Taking the seat next to Neil, she set a glass of water in front of him. "Are we comfy?"

We? Neil thought. Tiny word '*we*.' Truth be told, from the start he had pushed to the back of his mind the very possibility of the word 'we' as it applied to him and her—*together*. Her saying it out loud seemed to …

"There are things we need to bring out into the open," she said. "… things we need to discuss."

"What kind of things," he said as his heart skipped a beat. It seemed to do that every time she uttered *that* simple two-letter word. Why did it gallop like a spooked stallion now? Nuts!

"God is good, Neil. Christ is good. When people see us do right by them, whether they understand it or not, whether *you* understand it or not, they see Christ in what we do. We rack up witnesses every time we involve ourselves in the lives of others."

Oh, so she's back to that topic. Neil sighed in resignation. "You're right. We should stop butting in while we're ahead."

"That's not what I meant. Whether we like it or not, some people will see Christ in the good things *we* do. I think that's why Andrews called you a Trog. You feel insulted by that tag, don't you?"

"Yeah," Neil said in clear irritation.

"I hate the word, too, but that never stopped you from calling *me* that."

"Oh, I see." He looked squarely into her dark, almost black eyes and saw the hurt there. "Sorry, Ramona. I've been mean, haven't I?"

Chapter 15

The Escape

BILLY sat up abruptly. A noisy clank at the door said old fuzz-buckets was bringing dinner. What would it be tonight? Perhaps a thick, juicy Porterhouse cooked through and through with just a touch of pink inside, or maybe Lobster Florentine with a nice white sauce, or better yet …

The door swung open and in stepped the pirate. With a cruel smirk, he dropped a bowl in front of Billy, splattering some of its contents on the floor.

… Gruel. Yummy.

"Eat up, Cop. Want ya fit for farmin'."

"I felt the ship shake and jostle a bit. Get yourself into a scrape, did you?"

"Took on some fresh stock, we did. Twenty head or so."

"My … You're quite the entrepreneurs, aren't you? Everyone get a room to himself?"

"Oh, no, Enforcers is special." The pirate's deep blue eyes were loaded with hate and set to kill. "Most folks got a huge hankerin' to gut yer type in the middle of the night, and that greatly cuts down on our profits. Most folks in the trade jus' as soon set your types t'drift and call it square, but Cap turns a profit in spite of the problems y'all makes fer him."

"You don't sound like you agree with your

Captain."

"I says, behave yersef and live; don't and you die. It's jus' that simple." The pirate tossed a wood bit to the mattress.

Billy picked up the well-chewed stick and wondered how many mouths had clamped down on it. Had to be chock full of germs. "Do we have to test this collar every day? I'm so getting tired of this routine."

"Bite or break yer teeth, boy. Yer choice."

Billy bit down on the stick, and the pirate touched his wristlet. Billy bolted back and writhed as if the collar sent pain through his neck until the pirate released the trigger.

"Behave yersef, boy, and I'll let ya git some fresh air later t'day."

Billy pulled the bit from his mouth, tossed it to the pirate without looking, gathered his strength, and then strained to sit upright.

"Have we landed? Where are we?"

"We've made groundfall, but where abouts don't concern you none. We'll be leaving soon enough. Now eat yer meal fer it gets cold." With that the pirate turned and closed the door behind him.

Old fuzz-buckets, thought Billy. Carlton Ogier coined the name for Captain Avery, and yet it somehow fit this old pirate to a tee as well. Billy chuckled at the thought of Avery going rogue and becoming a pirate, *had he lived*. He tried to picture Avery dressed as this old coot. *Nah*, he thought. *Never happen*.

AFTER visiting Billy, Neil went to the galley where Ramona was waiting.

She carefully set a plate of what actually looked like real scrambled eggs on the breakfast bar for him. "So how is our guest?"

"Billy? He's a ham. Every time I make believe I'm triggering the dog collar, he pretends it works. His thrashing about like he's being shocked is almost comical, but I must say he's quite the actor. His overacting might fool a real pirate, but I think it's a little over the top to froth at the mouth like he does."

"So, is everything set?" Ramona said.

Neil glanced at the ceiling. "*Cel?*"

"Yes, sir. The holographic slaves will seem real to him, but are you sure Praxis is the right place to set him free?"

"It's as good a place as any. Billy's a credible witness and will testify of what he's seen. He thinks Ramona and I are dead, as well as the others. Ogier included."

"Now see," Ramona said, "that concerns me. What if Carl Ogier makes his way back to the Coalition of Planets? Won't that short-circuit Billy Taft's testimony ... and our alibi?"

"Honestly, Ramona, I think Carl wants no part of his past life. And besides, it's a big 'verse. What are the chances of those two ever running into each other again?"

"I hope you're right."

He and Ramona ate quietly; he trying to hide his own worry, she intent on working out her own issues.

As Neil leaned back and glanced out the large portal, a new thought popped into his head. Killing all those folks on the Princess was, all in itself, clearly wrong, and he had known it even before he let that first torpedo fly, but where did that belief originally come from? Was his own feelings or intellect trustworthy enough to weigh the value of human life? Was anyone's? Did there even exist a reliable gage to trust a man's life to? He shuttered.

Carl seemed to share his regrets, but Billy … he was a different story altogether. Like Troy, that young pilot seemed to take delight in killing; even looking forward to future events.

Neil stretched but didn't take his eyes from the window.

And then there was *Celestria*. Was she right in calling for Troy and Jessup's deaths? Could that same mindset be applied to Billy? Should it be? In light of the blood on his own hands, why was Neil excluded from her judgment? None of this made sense.

Beyond the window, and through the stand of trees at a distance, Neil saw a few deer grazing. At any given moment, at least one had its head up, alert to its surroundings.

Was it like that with *Celestria*? Was her head up, alert to dangers he couldn't see, protecting him?

But was the ship itself a threat? She, *Celestria*, had asked him to kill. Asked? No ... the ship was quite insistent. That dark side of *Celestria* had never been resolved in Neil's mind, and he didn't know what to do with it. One thing was certain; although he wanted to ask her about it, he was afraid of what he might learn.

After breakfast he and Ramona headed to the cargo bay. *Celestria* had filled it with holographic crates, boxes, and canisters such as would be found on a pirate ship. The wide bay door was open and formed a ramp to the grass-covered ground. Holographic people, "slaves" milling about, "guards" watching them, looked very real; real enough to fool Billy, at any rate. His focus would be on his escape, not on the others.

As Neil went down the hallway to fetch Billy, *Celestria* holographicly dressed him in pirate garb. Rapping once, he shouted, "Step back from the door."

Inside, Billy sat upright on the mattress with his back to the wall.

"Time to stretch yer legs, boy."

Billy scrambled to his feet, hesitated, and then cautiously passed the pirate to head out.

Neil followed Billy to the ramp and the younger man stepped out into the sun with a

113

hand cupped above his eyes until they adjusted to the day's light. The others there glanced up at him but otherwise paid him no attention.

Neil shoved him forward. "Stretch yer legs some, then git back aboard quick-like when I says. Got that?"

Billy stumbled, caught himself, and then nodded once. "I hear you."

With his hands shoved deep in his pockets, Billy walked casually through the crowd, nodding to some, ignoring others, but all the while working his way toward the tree line.

Neil let Billy get close enough to the trees so that he would have a reasonable chance to make his escape. "All right, scum," shouted Neil. "Back inside."

Billy bolted, ducked through the trees, and ran as fast as his sore legs could carry him. Chased by a few 'guards,' Billy stumbled, slid, and rolled into a bush-covered hole—panicked that he was trapped. Then he realized the luck he'd fallen into. The guards passed right over him. He heard them calling to one another until their voices faded into the distance.

He stayed put until he saw the ship lift off without him, then waited in that hole the entire day, just to slink away under the cover of night.

Stupid moons. Both were full.

Chapter 16
Carl Ogier

CELESTRIA arose from the forest to head for the sky. From the bridge Neil watched the treetops descend below the windows and vanish from view. Taking the ship a few hundred miles west, well clear of Billy Taft, he'd repeat the same ruse with Carlton Ogier. Not believing Carl enjoyed his enslavement, it was important to Neil to discover Carl's real intentions.

The ship landed amid the trees once again, lowered the cargo bay door/ramp and set the holographic people in place.

Neil led Carl out to give him an opportunity to run, but unlike William Taft, Carl turned to face his foe, uncoupled the collar, pulled it from his neck, and tossed it to his captor's feet.

"Day one I disabled that collar. It hasn't worked since."

Surprised, Neil studied Carl. "Seein' that collar is useless, ain't you goina run?"

"You promised passage to Providence. Why would I throw that away?"

Neil narrowed on Carl's face. "Life as a slave appeals to you, does it, boy?"

"Three squares and honest work on a farm appeals to me just fine. It's a step up from what I've been doin'. It's a good deal; you get paid for my passage, and I get a new start."

Neil glanced at Ramona, and, even through

115

her holographic disguise saw the puzzled look in her eyes. What was Neil going to do now? What could he do with that?

"*Celestria*, kill the slaves."

Carl stumbled back in surprise. "No! Wait! Give me a chance to—"

But before he could do more, the slaves that surrounded him vanished. That is, all but one young woman who stood to one side of the ramp.

Carl spun, looking all around, then turned back to the Brig's chief guard.

"*Celestria*, kill the guards as well," Neil said. And they, too, disappeared.

Now thoroughly bewildered, Carl, with mouth agape, stared at the pirate. "What's going on? Who *are* you people?"

Neil glanced at Ramona.

She nodded.

"*Cel*, kill our covers."

"Are you certain, Captain?"

Neil shot a fleeting look at Ramona once more. "*Cel* ... please."

"Aye, sir."

Their holographic overlays faded to leave nothing behind but Neil and Ramona as Carl had known them.

Stunned, the elation written across Carl's face was instantly recognizable.

"I can't believe this. Is it really you, Cap? You're alive?"

He rushed forward to clasp his former

Captain's hand. As he clapped Neil's shoulder, clear, excited eyes above a broad smile said he was genuinely grateful Neil and Ramona had survived.

Ramona stepped forward as he turned to her.

"And you ..." Carl reached out a friendly hand.

Brushing it aside, Ramona embraced the young officer. "Welcome aboard *Celestria*, Ensign."

Carl pushed back a little to consider her face. "You're the waitress from the Bush and Quail. I never caught your name, miss, but I am so glad to see you alive."

"Ramona ... or if you like, Mona will do. And thank you, Ensign, it's good to see you alive as well. So, my faith is all right with you?"

"I'd rather be a farmer than to have to enforce such stupid anti-religion laws, Mona."

"You really want to be a farmer, Carl?" Neil said.

Carl shrugged. "I got a choice?"

"Join us."

Barely able to contain his excitement, Carl hesitated in surprise. "What? Are you serious?"

"We could use a crewman with your abilities," Ramona said. "Whatta ya say? Join us?"

Carl stepped back to look at *Celestria*. "I would rather fly a million years with you in this old tub than spend another minute as an Enforcer."

"Well then," Ramona said, "you're hired."

Carl seemed unable to wipe the smile off his face. "If *freedom of religion* is part of the deal, Ramona, could you tell me about this faith of yours?"

"You betcha," she confirmed, and preceded the men back into the ship.

Neil wrapped a friendly arm around the younger man as they followed her. "Glad to have you at my wing, Carl. Let's keep flyin'."

A SHOWER, a room of his own, a seat on the bridge, and an enthusiastic Carl Ogier took his place among his new friends.

Celestria lifted off and headed out of Praxis' atmosphere undetected by Andrews or any of his people.

This was a new day. Carl would be taking orders from a waitress—well, former waitress—and that was fine with him. It was far more preferable than taking orders from a maniac like Lieutenant Troy Younger.

Somehow, the stars seemed brighter, the expanse of the Milky Way crisper, and his friends truer.

An orphan, Carl had no ties to the Coalition that mattered. Not even his life's savings sitting in a bank on Parandi was worth his attention.

With the promise of a great future, this was a new day indeed. Yes!

Chapter 17

Heaven's Mirror

NEIL stared into the coffin with blank eyes. This was just wrong. These wooden caskets were supposed to be for old people, not young boys …

… *not* for his best friend.

Twelve-year-old Neil felt his chin quiver, but the more he tried to stop it, the more it took on a life of its own.

Stupid government medical system was totally worthless. Why'd they let this happen? Even as tears gathered in his eyes to blur his vision, he reached in to take hold of a cold, lifeless hand.

"Neil!" his mother scolded.

"Let the child be, woman," his dad said. "Let him grieve his best friend's passing and say *good-by* however he wants."

Mrs. Avery sniffled. "He was precious to me, too. Dennis was a wonderful boy."

Precious? thought Neil. You saved my life, Dennis. Being at his funeral was hard, probably the hardest thing Neil had ever had to do.

Right then, Cindy stepped to Neil's side to rest a soft hand lightly on his shoulder. Neil wrapped an arm around his sweetheart and released Dennis' lifeless hand. She sobbed, he pulled her closer, and she pressed her face into his shoulder. His own tears streamed down his cheeks, and fell into her long, black hair, but he couldn't let go of his only tie to his onetime best friend. The three of them had been inseparable.

Looking back over his shoulder, Neil saw the people that filled the room; many wept, some held loved ones close, others chatted quietly. Why did this have to be real? He thought. Why did this have to *be*, at all?

He became aware of other mourners reaching out to him, pushing aside their own anguish to comfort the two adolescents.

Grammy Dugan, Dennis' grandmother, eased through the crowd to wrap trembling but warm arms around both children. Assaulted by a strong mix of menthol and eucalyptus, Neil held his breath, but didn't pull away.

"You two were his greatest joy," Grammy Dugan said. "You know that don't you? His last words were, 'Tell Cindy and Neil, I'm waiting. I'll be at heaven's gate to greet them.' You kids have been such a wonderful blessing to Mr. Dugan and me as well. Don't lose sight of that. Neither of you lose sight of that."

Like electricity fizzing through him, her words broke through his grief. Neil wrenched himself free and glared at the old lady. Anger seared away the numbness.

'Heaven's gate? Blessing?' Was *this* old woman a ... a Trog? Dennis, his best buddy in the whole world, was religious? How could Neil not have known? How could he have missed the signs? Perhaps he secretly knew, but saw that saying so would have cost him the friendship of a great guy.

Sick to his stomach and needing air, he pushed through the crowd to the door and hurried out of the house …

… but found himself standing on the deck of the *Emperor's Princess.*

Standing in the hallway, an adult Neil Avery faced his childhood friend, Dennis Dugan.

"Dennis, what are you doing here!"

Feeling betrayed, Neil caught his breath and stared at Dennis as if seeing him for the first time. "Dennis, you were loyal to me. You wouldn't duce me by keeping a secret this big and dangerous, no matter what. You're not a stinking narrow minded, finger pointing Trog. No way. Impossible, Neil thought. You're not here.

Blond and blue eyed, the young face morphed into that of Carl's. Then an explosion … the *Emperor's Princess* shook and rumbled in her first death throws … fire ran through the hallway … Dennis … Carl was consumed.

"Captain, wake up!" *Celestria's* quiet voice persisted.

Neil jerked awake. Though his mind was still hazy, reality slipped into place, and he realized that he still occupied his own bed aboard *Celestria*.

"Are you ill, Captain?"

Shaken, he let the last wisps of the memory fade, but didn't answer.

"Were you dreaming?"

He threw back the sweat-soaked sheets, sat up on the edge of the bed, and speared trembling hands though his hair.

"Nightmare, Captain?"

With a voice raspy from interrupted sleep, Neil guardedly answered, "More like buried memories forced to the surface, *Cel*. All these years ..."

Neil rubbed his face hard to wake himself. "I forgot Dennis, my childhood best friend, was a ..." but he stopped short of saying the epithet out loud.

Celestria's calm voice broke the long moment of silence. "A Christian, Capt. Avery?"

"A Trog," Neil snapped, before taking another minute to calm his tone. "We called believers, Trogs."

"And his family? Were they believers as well, sir?"

Neil took a deep breath. "More than likely, *Cel*."

"Capt. Avery, did you turn them in?"

Neil halfheartedly shook his head. "No. He died of cancer when he was twelve. I suppose I pushed aside the idea of Carl being a Tro ..."

Neil faltered.

"... a believer."

"I'm sorry, Captain. Didn't you mean Dennis?"

"Dennis. Yes, Dennis. I'm sorry." Tears welled but, by sheer strength of will, he held them back.

"In my dream I saw young Dennis aboard the *Emperor's Princess* the day I downed her. Do you understand what I'm saying, *Cel*? My very best friend in the whole world ... I killed him ... *I did*."

"Sir, it was just a dream. He wasn't there."

"He might as well have been, *Celestria*. By killing that ship, I killed Carl ... just as if he had walked those decks himself."

"Sir. That is the second time you've substituted Dennis' name with Carl's."

"What? Did I?"

Jumping to his feet, Neil showered, dressed, and remade his bed with fresh sheets.

Then, in the watchless hours, cool and quiet, in an effort to walk away from his memories, Neil headed to the galley in search of warm milk to help him sleep. Fighting exhaustion, but not calling for the iris door, he stumbled through the halls, and down the stairs to find the galley.

Neil shook himself. Eerily alike, did he actually see blond, blue-eyed Carl as an adult Dennis? Was this the reason, from day one, Carl had bothered him ... and the reason he trusted the young pilot at his wing?

If he could just put the image of Carl out of his mind, thought Neil, then he caught himself. Why now did the image of Carl insist on replacing that of Dennis? Maybe there were real reasons his childhood invaded his dreams *now*, after all these years.

Dennis Dugan succumbed to cancer at age twelve, and though such things were common in the Coalition, it just didn't seem right that one of "God's chosen" should have passed away like that, if God was real.

If God's Word was true, then why did this image come to shake him from his bed? Had it come, by design, to bring Neil to his knees?

In the dark, Neil sat on the couch to ponder as he sipped the mug of warm milk. A Christian died. Why did that strike him as unusual? When he and his marauders swooped in on the *Princess*, why didn't God warn the Christians of the approaching danger? Neil couldn't put his finger on any real reason that made sense ... if God was real.

Thoughts of his sitting comfortably in his *Dart* diving on the liner forced their way into his mind. Although he was the one firing one torpedo after the next—*sickening*—it seemed like someone else's hand on the trigger.

Watching the slaughter of bodies blown into space, Neil felt numb. Without call, a lone tear stole down his cheek. He wiped it away with his fingers, then studied the moisture, mystified that it was there.

If coming to this so-called compassionate God afforded no one any greater protection from calamity, then why be a Christian at all?

Ramona said Jesus came to free people from sin, but was that it? Was that all there was to a life in Christ?

Wouldn't it have been smarter to have let Dennis live to preach and bring others to Christ? If God is Love, then where was the Love in letting a child suffer with cancer … and die?

And here sat Neil, guilty of murder, surrounded in comfort by an ancient, yet beyond modern spacecraft supposedly given him by the Great God of Heaven and Earth, Himself. Where was the justice in that?

"*Celestria*?"

"Yes, Master Avery."

"When we reach Providence Prime, I'll get off to find my own way back to Atheron. Watch over Ramona, will ya?"

"I don't think so!" Ramona's stern rebuttal came from the doorway. Dressed in a quilted robe over a shimmery nightgown, the hall's nightlights illuminated her form well enough for Neil to see her firm stance. Arms folded, she stood just inside the room's permanent entrance and glared at Neil, as anger infused her words. "What makes you think this ship isn't yours just as much as she's mine? Didn't you suffer the genetic alterations, Neil? Don't you think that *changed* you *permanently*?"

"Yeah, well …"

"We don't know the full effect of those alterations, now do we? Do you think you can even exist *without Celestria*?"

"Well, no. I …"

"Didn't you rescue the two life pods? Didn't you pilot us through Captain Andrew's fiasco? Could either *Celestria* or I alone, or either of us together, for that matter, have done that without you? This is where you belong, Mister, and don't *you* think otherwise."

Neil pushed himself to his feet and went to her. "I've done awful things, Ramona. You've seen the hashes on my helmet—the high count. You know what they mean. It was my job to kill Christians, remember?"

"Oh, stop with the self recriminations!" Raising her chin, she assumed a dignity that startled him and robbed him of any defense. "I don't remember your doing those horrible things, Mr. Avery."

"Well, regardless of your inability to recall the obvious, things need to be rectified."

"My memory is fine, Mr. Avery. Just as my Lord has done, I *choose* to forget the sins that He has forgiven. Your job is to do the same and put them behind you once and for all. You did this for Troy Younger; now give yourself the same grace."

Neil stiffened. "How can I forget things that flood my dreams and shake me from my sleep? If I'm ever to have peace, I must go back and face my past."

Ramona's eyes held a determination that seemed to see straight through to his heart.

"You and your one track mind," she snapped. "Face your past? You are to face your future, and see yourself as God sees you, Mr. Neil Avery. I realize that all this is new to you, and that it will take you a while to get your head around the truth. Sometimes the simplest principle is the most challenging, so let me give you a clue."

He focused. "Yeah? I'm listening."

Ramona tempered her tone. "To properly love others, you must first love yourself, Neil. It's just that simple." Having said that, she turned and headed away.

Neil watched her disappear into the shadows of the hallway. "Love myself? Who doesn't love himself?"

"She's right, Captain Avery," *Celestria* said. "You don't love yourself." Usually Celestria's voice had a universal quality to it as if coming from everywhere. This time it came from directly behind him.

Neil turned, and jerked with surprise. Before him stood a six-foot tall ghostly figure of a woman. He stared, transfixed.

"Celestria?"

Her stature, though obviously feminine, was regal. Her flowing floor length gown was an almost blinding iridescent white, yet he could bear it easily. Golden hair hung in cascading curls about her shoulders and held the same colors as the broad cloth belt that girded her waist. A gold cross, hanging from a chain, rested lightly on her chest. He touched her shoulder—she was real.

"In the confines of this ship, sir, I do have substance, such as it is. But back to the point, Capt. French is right. You don't love yourself."

Neil took a deep breath to regain his composure before addressing the vision before him. "Maybe I don't like the guy I see in the mirror. I hope to change that by going back to Atheron. I want to be a Dennis Dugan, a selfless, honorable man."

"No, sir." Her voice held an uncompromising austerity. "The universe has had its Dennis Dugan, and for the appropriate amount of time. What the universe lacks now, and is waiting for, is a proper Neil Avery. You won't find him reflected in some man-made martyrdom but in Heaven's mirror."

"Heaven's mirror?"

"When you see yourself in Heaven's mirror, you'll know who you are and what you should do. Until then, you'll impress no one but yourself with your self-styled acts of nobility."

"So where do I find this Heaven's mirror you speak of?"

Celestria raised an eyebrow as if to say the answer was obvious, and then motioned toward the doorway. "Who you really are is reflected in Ramona's eyes. You just haven't noticed."

Chapter 18

The Shuttle

NEIL turned from the door to *Celestria*. "Should I go to her now?"

"No, sir. You should go to the bridge." The avatar's image faded into the dark.

Setting his cup in the sink, Neil turned to a bare wall. "Bridge."

The wall irised open. Beyond it, the bridge was lit only by the consoles. The air was cool and except for the faint dutiful hum of a few instruments, the room was quiet.

He slipped into the pilot's seat half checking the scanner before noticing the faint blip. "Well, what do we have here?" he mumbled to himself. "What's this dead ahead?"

Neil zeroed the scanner, narrowing in on the object. What's a shuttle doing way out here? he thought. Suddenly two more blips entered the screen heading at high speed toward the smaller.

"Full speed, *Cel*. Give me all you've got." Once within range, the scanner started tagging the blips with I.D. numbers, identifying two corsairs pursuing the shuttle.

Neil cursed and hit the com. "Ramona, Carl, to the bridge. Pirates!"

It looked as though two pirates had caught a short-range shuttle off guard, blocking its way home, and were now chasing it out and away from the safety of police and patrols.

The portal dilated and in stepped Carl. A moment later Ramona came through the iris from a different direction than had Carl. Neil spun his seat to face them.

"Pirates have blocked a shuttle's escape. They'll reach it before we do. Suggestions?"

"Looks like we've got a fight on our hands," Ramona said. "I say we give 'em a showing they won't soon forget."

"Agreed, Cap," Carl said.

"Neil, we'll man the guns. Get *Celestria* between that shuttle and those pirates as soon as you can. Looks like you'll have your hands full, but your piloting is our best chance to beat them."

Neil nodded and turned back to the screen. "Hang on to your seats. We're going in."

Carl took aim and pulled the trigger, but at this distance the plasma charged two-pounders did little more than distract the pirates, yet it was enough to give the shuttle occupants hope and to see that help was on the way.

The pirates reached their prey and, to knock out its defenses, started hitting it with ion shield-busters.

Defiantly, the unarmed shuttle turned and dodged between the corsairs in an effort to turn their own guns against them.

"Cheeky move," mumbled Neil. By the shuttle's old-school maneuvers and by the way it turned and dodged well beyond the craft's design limits, Neil guessed its Captain was once a *Wasp* pilot, a military man. Even if the pirates never connected, if its pilot kept this up, the shuttle would soon tear itself apart.

"Hang tight, bud. We're almost there."

Suddenly one corsair's shot clipped the shuttle and sent it spinning, careening out of control. When a second shot tagged it, the shuttle began to spew smoke into space.

Carl fired and kept firing as Ramona released several rockets. The pirates started taking blows and turned to address *Celestria* to see what she could give them.

The shuttle, dead and adrift, was spitting fuel and flames.

Neil cut between the corsairs and headed for the shuttle as Carl and Ramona heated the guns.

"Scanner readings look grim," Neil said.

"Never too late," Carl said. "Get us beside her! Mona take the guns." He called for the cargo bay and dived through the iris before it fully opened.

Neil brought *Celestria* up next to the shuttle, tractored it in close, and extended *Celestria's* shields around it. "*Cel*, give me the cargo bay and take the helm," he said. Jumping to his feet, he bolted through the iris.

At the bay's open door sat the shuttle. From its open hatch, smoke billowed into *Celestria*.

From the smoke, Carl dragged the pilot into *Celestria* and Neil dropped to perform CPR on the unconscious man.

"*Celestria*," Carl said, "jettison the shuttle

and vent this smoke."

"Negative, Ensign. I detect two more life signs."

Celestria jolted and rumbled as the pirates began to fire on her.

Carl took a deep breath and hurried back into the thick black smoke.

Neil kept his compressions to a steady pace, even though his mind was divided between the pirate threat, Ramona on the bridge, Carl in the burning shuttle, and the pilot beneath his hands.

Suddenly the man gasped in air on his own, then collapsed into a coughing fit. As soon as he could breathe again, the man reached out toward the shuttle. "My wife. My baby …"

The ship jerked hard again. A sudden piercing scream from the shuttle sent a cold jolt up Neil's spine.

As he stood, the ship bucked, knocking him to the floor. He scrambled to his feet, stumbled, and then shot toward the shuttle's hatchway.

Carl dragged a woman, still clutching her baby, from the ship. His right arm and shoulder, seared and blistered, hung limp at his side, but he didn't let go of the woman with his good arm until he had her well clear of the smoke and flames.

Neil eased her to the floor.

Then Carl collapsed.

Chapter 19

The Hospital

CARL forced open heavy eyelids and blinked to clear his blurred vision.

To his left sat a machine, which beeped and flickered, and from which some clear fluid flowed through tubes taped to his wrist. His right shoulder and arm, heavily bandaged, ached and were beginning to burn.

Reading magazines, Ramona and Neil, sat nearby to his right. Carl felt an errant irresponsible bubble of laughter rise, but it stayed captive in his throat. He mentally shook his head at the incongruity. Ramona read *Shipbuilder's Yearly*, as Neil thumbed through *Modern Bride*. Behind them, through a window into the hallway, he could see nurses at their duty stations.

Mona looked up, jumped to her feet, and took his hand. "Hey. Hi, you." Her hands were warm and as soft as silk. Her smile, though happy, held more than a touch of concern.

"What happened? Where am I?" Carl asked, his voice a faint raspy whisper.

Neil stepped next to Mona. "You're going to be all right, Carl. You're in a hospital on Delta Omicron 4."

Despite his body's discomfort and the growing pain in his shoulder, Carl became aware of a serious detail that had escaped him earlier. He noticed how well Mona and Cap seemed to fit as a couple, and wondered if either could see they belonged together.

Wanting to take Neil's hand, he tried to reach, but a stabbing anguish shot through his arm. He screamed as pain pushed everything else aside to demand immediate attention.

"Nurse!" he heard someone shout as he writhed in agony. And then, just as suddenly as it began, the torture melted away, pushed back like a receding tide.

A nurse now stood near the machine. "I'm sorry, Mr. Thunburry. This old med-tech machine glitches now and again. I'll get maintenance up here right away." She hurried out.

Carl took a deep, shaky breath and tried to relax. Now the concern in both of his friends' eyes wasn't hidden in the least.

"Come on now. You said I was okay, so knock off the grim faces already."

Neil gently held Carl's bandaged hand. "I just hate to see you hurt, buddy."

Carl forced a smile. "So? Did they make it?"

"They? Oh, the Protmeyers." Mona said. "Yep. Just a little smoke inhalation. All three will be up and about in no time. You're quite the hero, running into a burning shuttle like that."

Carl tucked his uninjured hand behind his neck and studied the ceiling. "Three thousand twenty one. Good."

"What?" Mona looked at Neil for some kind of explanation, but he only shook his head and shrugged.

"Three thousand … what's that about, Carl?" Ramona said.

Carl looked away toward the window. "It's nothing. I keep having these disconnected thoughts drop into my head. Must be the pain medication talking."

"Three thousand twenty one," Neil said, "and three makes three thousand twenty four. Isn't that right, Carl?"

"Does it?" Although a blue, cloudless sky gave him nothing to see, Carl didn't take his eyes from the window.

"What?" Ramona's question said she didn't like being left out of the loop. Neil had guessed Carl's slip of the tongue, and Carl hoped he'd be smart and just drop it.

Neil patted Carl's leg in understanding, turned, and left the room without saying more.

"Tell me, Carl, what's the significance of that number."

He turned to consider her face, a mix of frustration and worry, but he ignored her question. "So, what do the doctors say about my arm? How long will I be here?

The subject seemed to hit her hard. As her eyes suddenly filled with tears, she blinked hard to keep them from falling. Mona swallowed and tried to speak, but the words appeared to catch in her throat. Looking everywhere but at Carl, she fidgeted and fussed as if she didn't know what to do with her hands, smoothing the bedspread and fluffing his pillow a little.

"Will you stop?" Carl grabbed her wrist with his good hand and met her eyes. It was obvious she was holding back bad news.

"What did the doctors say, Mona? Tell me."

Not wanting to answer, she shook her head and tried to pull away, but Carl held her.

"Tell me!"

Her chin quivered and her eyes released a stream of tears.

"Let her go, Carl." Neil spoke quietly from the doorway. "I'll tell you everything; just let Ramona go."

He released a long breath. Now that Neil was willing to say, Carl no longer wanted to hear. He knew what was coming. No one had to hit him in the head with a brick, and that's exactly what he felt was now flying straight at him. "Never mind."

"Two days ago, you saved three people, Carl. Don't lose sight of that."

"I lost the use of my arm, didn't I? Well, there's justice for you."

"Carl, you saved three—"

"Yeah! You just said that. Only a lousy little three thousand twenty one left to go." Disgust distorted Carl's face as he snapped his head back toward the window.

"What?" Mona said. "What's with that number you keep repeating? What does it have to do with anything?"

From behind, Neil placed a gentle hand on her shoulder. "The people on board the *Princess* numbered—"

"Three thousand twenty four." Ramona interrupted. "Oh, I see. Is that what that rescue was all about, Carl? You're trying to set right the wrong you committed? You think with a bum arm you can't save more lives?"

Carl turned to glare at her. "Yeah, well … how else do you set right a wrong, Mona?"

"Oh." Neil took his seat and jostled the stack of magazines with a tense hand. "So you're bothered more by the inability to make amends than by the loss of your arm, huh?"

Her cheeks wet with tears, Mona stepped forward and slapped Carl's face hard. "You idiot!"

Stunned, Carl looked up at intense eyes. "Ouch, woman. That hurt."

She leaned over his bed until she was just inches from his nose. "So, you either have to rescue people or get yourself killed to pay for your crimes, is that it? Well, let me make something crystal clear to you. I told you, it doesn't work that way. Even if you manage to save a million people it wouldn't set things right. Only forgiveness will do that, so listen up. You stop trying to get yourself killed starting now, Mister, or so help me I'll … I'll …"

Carl smiled mischievously. "Kill me?"

Now at a complete loss for words, Mona

hesitated.

With a slight tilt of his chin, Carl pecked the tip of her nose with a kiss. "If you cared more, I'd be in *real* trouble."

She leaned further and hugged him tightly.

With his good arm, Carl returned her embrace the best he could. Never before had he felt like this toward anyone.

"We love you, Carl. I love you. Don't you ever try to leave us again, you foolish man." Mona pulled back and wiped her cheeks with the back of her hand.

She's amazing, thought Carl. There was no wondering why Neil had fallen for her as he had. Carl felt himself drawn to her as well. Avoiding her eyes, he looked away.

A sister, think of her as a sister, he told himself, frantic to rein in his galloping emotions. There's got to be a way to see her as a sister.

He glanced at Neil and recognized the look in the man's expression. Uh oh, Neil knew. Neil saw it in his eyes and knew.

Carl looked away. "You two can go on without me. I think it would be best if you did."

Neil half moaned, half growled before speaking. "Not going to happen, Carl. There's more to this than you think. When we leave here, we leave together, Ramona, me, and *you*, and I'll hear no more about it."

Mona sniffled and half pointed to Neil. "What he said, Mister."

Carl let his face relax into a natural, easy smile while he crammed his renegade emotions into a mental box and locked the lid on tight. He didn't understand how all this was going to unfold in a positive manner. But one thing was becoming clear. He did belong with these two people—*for now, anyway*—resigning to the truth forging itself into his brain. When he was with them, he was home.

"So, then," he said, changing the subject to lighten the mood, "what did that nurse call me? Tudberry?"

"Thunburry," Neil said as he glanced at the door. "We haven't crossed the border, so let's not—"

"Say no more, Neil. I get it."

Mona stepped from the room and went to the nurse's station to get tissues. Through the glass, Carl watched her dry her tears and blow her nose.

"Falling for the girl, I see," Neil said reopening the subject Carl wanted closed.

Carl let his gaze drop from the window to Neil's watchful eyes. "What? No, no, … I see her more as a sister—"

Neil scoffed. "Yeah, right. Look, I see the way you watch her. You're falling in love with her, and you can't help it, can you?"

"Neil, come on." Carl turned away as if to look outside, but the image in his mind of Mona's warm smile drowned out reason's voice. "It's plain you two are an item. I'm not going to—"

"Ramona and I? No, man. You got it wrong. She and I merely co-captain *Celestria*, nothing more."

Carl coughed to clear his throat, then laughed. "Co-captains, huh? Man, you are so blind."

"What are you saying, that we're both in love with the same girl?

"Yeah. Maybe I should just stay here after all." Carl turned to the window. At present facing Neil was impossible. "Neil, how do *you* intend on making amends?"

For the longest moment, the machines' beeping was all that broke the silence.

"I've been thinking about returning to Atheron," Neil said at long last.

"What?" Carl glanced back at Neil who now had his chin down on his chest as he stared at the floor. "Why would you go back there?"

"Oh … to turn myself over to the … those people."

"Those people?"

"Trogs … to stand trial for what I've done."

Carl shook his head in disbelief. "We really do make a strange pair, don't we?"

"Look, Carl. I see no way past this, so I want you to take care of Ramona."

"I beg your pardon?" Mona's voice snapped Carl's attention back to the doorway. She stepped into the room, grabbed Neil by the collar, and yanked him to his feet with her own strength. Because he was taller than she, he was hunched over as she forced him to meet her eye to eye.

"You've tried to assign me to someone's care before. I'll have you know, Mr. Avery, I am not some painting to admire for a while and then just give away." Her grip, as she snugged his collar ends together, turned her knuckles white. "I said this before, too, and it's time you heard me! I am a person, Mister, an independent person with my own feelings, my own desires, and my own destiny. Don't you dare think you have the right to pass me around like some pretty flower."

She shoved him back into his chair and stormed out of the room.

Stunned, both men looked at each other in wide-eyed disbelief.

"She's all yours," Neil said in a panic. "I won't come betw—"

"No, no," Carl said. "I'll not stand in your way, my friend. Lovely woman, that. And she's all yours."

Just then two Enforcers entered the room.

Neil stood to his feet to confront them.

"Out of the way, Mister," said the ranking officer. "We need to question this man."

Neil, standing between them and Carl, didn't budge. "Leave him be. I'll answer your questions."

The officer raised his M-1-AH Mouser and pressed it into Neil's throat.

Neil didn't give way, but instead, spoke with a calm, unshaken voice. "Pull the trigger or lower the gun, but I'll not move, friend."

"What are you doing?" came a new voice from the door. In stepped the man Carl had rescued.

"Sorry, sir," the Enforcer said, pointing his gun at Carl. "This man is using a fictitious name. I suspect he's a Trog."

Now there's irony for you, thought Carl.

"Nonsense. Now get out of here," said the newcomer.

"I'm sorry, Mr. Protmeyer, but I have standing orders from the Consul himself."

Neil placed a hand on the Enforcer's shoulder and stepped forward. Off balance, the man had to move toward where Neil wanted him to go, out of the door. "I can explain, officer, but only in private." Neil pressed the soldier toward the hallway, but the man resisted.

"Please," Neil coaxed.

In order to preserve his dignity, the officer, with a slight tilt of the head, consented, and stepped into the hallway, but away from the nurses' station and the people there.

Neil leaned forward to speak quietly into the enforcer's ear. "That's Headley Farnsworth the third. If his dad were to find out he risked his own life to rescue a commoner ..."

"Mr. Protmeyer isn't a commoner, pal," said the officer. "He's Proctor Protmeyer's brother."

The officer's face, smug and full of conceit,

reflected who Neil used to be. For years, without thought, Neil had acted just like this idiot. Without warning an intense anger filled Neil, and in that instant, he wanted nothing more than to slap the man's fool attitude clean off his face and shake some sense into him. Neil's training came to his rescue and he managed to stay calm, keeping his feelings out of his face.

"The Proctor?" Neil glanced back at the room as if to keep his words secret. "Worse yet, Captain. If daddy hears about his son—even about his being aboard an old freighter like mine —there'll be fall out like you've never seen."

"So? What's that to me? I've got to let the chips fall where—"

"They may?" Neil interrupted. "I don't think you want that. The Coalition tends to shoot the messenger. Everybody involved will be caught up in this, even if that person were an innocent, dutiful soldier just doing his job. Best to let things settle until a certain person is well away from the situation, don't you think?"

Suspicious, the Enforcer shook his head. "I've got to run him in. I have my orders."

"Come on, man. It's enough that the kid has to explain his scarred arm to his daddy, the Consul's First Council, but to have it come out that the boy is gallivanting around the universe in my old tub, it would kill the old man." Neil pointed to Carl's room. "As far as anyone knows, that young man is Carlos Thunburry, okay? Better for everybody, don't you think?"

The Enforcer looked toward Carl's room. "Frappin rich people sculking about like kids playing hooky." He shook his head in disgust. "Yeah, sure. Just keep him out of trouble."

"Yeah, man, don't you know it!"

Both men returned to the room just as Protmeyer was leaving. The Enforcer collected his partner, glanced at Carl, and then headed out.

"Do you know who that was?" Carl said. "The man I rescued?

"If I were to guess," Neil said, "I'd say the brother of Delta Omicron Four's chancellor, perhaps. But I could be wrong."

Carl laughed. "The guy wanted to hire me as his own personal bodyguard."

"Well?"

"Well what?"

"You going to take his offer?"

Carl dropped his gaze, his face sobered.

"Well, no, chief," Carl said.

"What? Why not?"

"After I explained my arm to him, he couldn't retract his offer fast enough. He almost ran to get out of here."

From deep concern, Neil's face changed. "Well, good," he said with a satisfied smile.

Carl shot an angry look at Neil, and then looked out the window to ignore Neil altogether.

"Had you accepted his offer, Carl, had he hired you away, Ramona and I would have had to risk our lives to convince you to reconsider. You belong with us, Carl."

Carl turned to look at Neil with a calloused eye. "What 'us' are you talking about? I thought your aim was to get yourself hanged. Weren't you going to Atheron to face trial?" He turned back to the window.

Neil studied Carl's pained expression and slowly began to realize that God might have Neil make amends in other ways.

Nothing in him wanted to abandon his young friend—*he wouldn't*—but what more could he say or do to help matters?

Maybe Carl was right, and his way of making amends was the precise way to get the job done. Between the two of them they'd have to save six-thousand forty-eight souls. If he dedicated the next hundred years to the task, he'd have to save sixty-five souls a year. If he could just figure out where to start, that just might be *doable.*

Well, he thought, he had time.

Neil froze.

A hidden genetic memory just popped to the surface. He suddenly knew both he and Ramona would live six to nine hundred years because of what *Celestria* had done, *if* he didn't get himself killed in the meantime.

Pushing that astonishing notion aside for later consideration, Neil refocused on Carl. As it was, Neil felt that the more he said to Carl, the more he made matters worse.

What a mess, Neil thought. All of this is beyond me. I need to talk to someone smarter. Maybe *Celestria* can help me sort this out.

Wait a minute. Ramona told him to let God prove Himself. Fine. Since I need the advice and guidance of someone smarter than me …

Feeling as if he were climbing way out on a very thin limb, Neil took a deep breath, his lips parted, but nothing came out. Praying suddenly seemed incredibly stupid.

He glanced around.

Fine.

"God, if You're there, and You've got this all figured out, then how about cluing me in?"

Chapter 20

The Addict

THE next day Neil, with Ramona at his side, entered Carl's hospital room with a glidechair.

Carl glanced at the couple, at the hovering chair, and then turned once again to the window ignoring them.

"Come on, Carl," Neil said. "Let's get out of this morgue."

Carl sighed, giving a slight shake of his head. "You two go on without me."

Humming cheerfully, Ramona came around the bed and shut off the machine.

"Hey, I need that!"

"Not anymore," she said brightly as she yanked the I.V. from his arm. She quickly placed a small bandage over the needle's insertion point. "Okay, he's ready. Let's do it."

Neil grabbed Carl by his good arm and pulled him abruptly from the bed and over his shoulders. "Let's go, pal. *Celestria's* waiting."

Neil spun, kicked the hover-chair to one side, carefully ducked Carl under the doorframe, and headed toward the stairwell as a frantic nurse called for security. An alarm horn squalled in unison with pulsing lights. Ignoring them, Neil and Ramona took the stairs to the roof.

Celestria, disguised as *Dangerous Haul*,

waited at the building's edge. Ramona hurried ahead, running up the ship's ramp and out of sight in record time. Slowed down by Carl's weight, Neil had only carried the young man halfway across the roof to the ship when behind them the door burst open again. Neil turned to see two security guards rush out with guns drawn.

"Good day, gentlemen," Neil called out. "Sorry, no time to chat, but tell the nurses for us that their services were greatly appreciated."

"Put that man down or I'll shoot," said one guard.

Neil smiled. "So shoot, already! What are you waiting for, an engraved invitation?"

The guard raised his gun to take careful aim.

Neil casually turned back to *Celestria*, to the awaiting ramp, and started toward it.

The guard fired, but the bullets glanced harmlessly off *Celestria's* enveloping shields.

Neil stepped aboard, turned back to the guards, and waved good-bye with his free hand.

Celestria retracted the ramp, closed the door, and headed for space.

"Let me down," Carl huffed.

"You going to behave?" Neil said.

"My shoulder! I need my …"

Ramona stepped in front of Carl, who hung draped over Neil's shoulder like a sack of potatoes, and shook a bottle of pills.

"What's that?"

"You going to behave?" She rattled the

bottle again.

Carl went limp and mumbled, "I'll be good, Mona. Can I please have something for the pain?"

"You want to try walking to your room," Neil said, "or shall I carry you all the way?"

"No, Cap. I can walk. Just put me down."

Before Neil could set Carl on his feet, Carl tried to snatch the pill bottle from Ramona.

She jerked it away. "Nope! Just one at a time, pal. These things are addictive, so I'll watch your dosage, if you don't mind."

Carl scowled. "I'll mind my own dosage, thank you very much. I'm all grown up now, … *Mom*."

"You ain't so big I can't take you over my knee, *son*. You mind yourself, and I'll mind the pills. Got it?"

She was only twenty-one, just a year older than Carl, but Neil felt as though her take on the situation was right. The squabbling brat still draped across his shoulders needed looking after, not free reign.

"Come on, kid," Neil said. "Play nice."

"Are you going to let me down?"

Neil shrugged and set him gingerly on the deck.

"I'll take that pill now," Carl said.

Ramona popped the cap from the bottle, jostled one pill into the cap, and dumped it from the lid into his eager hand. Carl moved swiftly down the hall to the galley and water.

Staring after the boy as he hurried away, Neil sighed and glanced toward Ramona, a worried look in his eyes. "I hate seeing him like this."

"I know. He seems more eager for the drug than the pain would warrant."

"It is more than just the pain. You're a captivating lady."

"Well, if he begins to think of me as Mom, that will give him a legitimate label to slap on his emotions, at least for a while. He needs some stability in his relationships, and I don't think God would have put Carl with us if He didn't have a plan that would remove the confusion. Things will work out."

She moved next to him and tucked a hand under Neil's arm, then rested her head on his shoulder in a semi-embrace. Neil didn't know how to handle her closeness any more than Carl had. He searched for a safe topic.

"I've seen firsthand what the Coalition's medical system can do, or rather, what it doesn't do." He patted her hand. "Had Carl stayed in that hospital much longer ..."

"He's certainly better off with us," Ramona agreed.

"If we can get him to Providence, *its* medical system may be better, or at least they might be willing to give reconstructive surgery a shot. *Celestria*, keep a constant watch on Carl's vitals will you, and let Ramona know if and when he truly needs his meds, okay?"

"Aye, sir."

Ramona stretched up to kiss Neil's cheek. "You really are a great guy. You know that?"

Neil considered the sincerity of her smile. How he wanted to believe her, but his own jumbled feelings, left him bewildered. It was probably best to not answer the invitation in her smile until he had sorted out his own mind.

He had no desire to leave the comfort of her arms, but he knew in time he'd have to completely surrender everything to those he'd wronged. That was the right thing to do, the *only* thing to do, and perhaps his losing her all in itself was the very thing her God considered payment for his deeds. Perhaps—*perhaps not*—but payment had to be made regardless.

"Tell you what, Ramona. You pilot us out of this system while I prepare lunch. I don't think you've seen as much of the bridge as you would've liked."

Dissatisfaction morphed her smile into a scowl.

Suddenly self-conscious, he spun on his heel without another word, and stiffly headed away. cursing his stupid response and wished Ramona didn't have the ability to jostle him like this. He released a long anxious breath, irritated with himself. As he neared the exit he stopped to look back.

Ramona stood motionless, just watching him walk away. The hurt in her eyes tugged at his heart, and stopped him cold.

Internally, Neil shook himself. Was this just some strange infatuation he had with what he had been denied, forbidden fruit, a Trog?

Trog … He nearly choked on the word that left a dry bitter taste in his mouth.

Did Ramona portray a realistic picture of what a believer was? Was she what Christians were truly like? Or was he blinded by something else, his own unguarded feelings perhaps?

Before he met her, back when he was a clear thinking man, the platitude "out from under a rock Troglodyte," made perfect sense when applied to a finger pointing religious zealot. But it certainly didn't fit when referring to her.

She took a step toward him, and in response, as if on autopilot, his body turned and stepped toward her as though *it* knew better than he.

Everything important to him was embodied in her. In that instant he no longer cared about his own ego, his ever-present desire to appear manly and in control, nor about returning to Atheron, to the Christians there, to satisfy his sense of justice. Right then, the only thing in his field of concentration was what awaited him on the other side of the cargo bay.

And when they finally came together, to hold each other, to share each other's affection and concerns, his heart pounded in his chest, but unlike any other time in his life, it seemed to hit like a hammer beating imperfections out of red-hot iron. Neil realized something new had been forged here; something that stood at odds with his own view of himself, and his sense of right and wrong. In opposition to his plans, it was clear now that here, in her arms, was where he belonged.

Neil relaxed tense muscles and let his cheek rest in Ramona's soft, sweet smelling hair; and now, with Ramona in his arms, he finally saw things differently. There was only one true way to square his attachment to her with his sense of justice. The deeper truth at work here seemed such an easy thing to lay a finger to that he wondered how he missed it earlier. He didn't know when, but sometime in the middle of this mess, amid the battles, the rescues, the quiet times at the table, a bond had formed between them; a bond that should continue if he was ever to set his life to rights.

A return to Atheron would cost him more than he was willing to pay. It would cost him her. And if he let that happen—knowing what it was like to be loved by her, to be touched by her, to hear her voice, to share her troubles and joy … and then to lose it all—dying would seem like no punishment at all in comparison.

Neil ground his teeth at the very thought.

The clean scent of her hair, the softness of it against his cheek without warning drew him back to where he was, and he felt himself relax in her embrace.

Tomorrow's worries faded, and for once, no longer pulled in two opposite directions, he consciously enjoyed the moment.

"I love you."

The proclamation fell from his lips all on its own, and in saying it, Neil felt detached as though someone else had said those three tiny but very important words. If someone else had brought those words to the surface on his behalf, then good—he was grateful. When it came to her, he was a hopeless addict.

Chapter 21
The Friend

NEIL opened his eyes to a brightening room. *Celestria's* way of waking him was to bring the lights up slowly to mimic sunrise. The air was fresh and crisp like an outing in the woods. It was always peaceful and pleasant, but this morning seemed even better.

He sat up and stretched, feeling as though for the first time in his life it was good to be alive. No bad dreams, no anxiety as to what the day might bring; just an expectation of good things to come. He showered, dressed, and headed upstairs to the bridge, which was now well lit and ready for him. Except for a few instruments' faint hum, the room was quiet.

Amused by *Celestria's* ability to set the perfect mood, he chuckled. Even the turned pilot's chair was inviting. He took it and half checked the scanner before noticing the faint blip, which brought him upright. "Well, what do we have here? A lifepod dead ahead? *Cel*, do you see this?"

"Aye. One life sign but readings are faint."

Neil zeroed the scanner to check his location. We're in the middle of Starry Decisis, he thought. Nowhere near traffic lanes. What's a lifepod doing way out here?

"*Cel*, bring us up beside the escape pod and draw it into the cargo bay, please. And take the bridge."

He stood and turned. "Cargo bay." The portal appeared and Neil stepped through. The bay door was already open, with the lifepod moving into position beside the ship. *Celestria* tractored it in and set the pod on the floor with remarkable care. The pod's cold skin began to coat with frost.

"*Cel*, pop the hatch."

With a sucking hiss, the pod's icy hatch pushed out from the pod and slid to one side. Neil reached in to the bearded man slumped in his seat. A strong pulse. Good.

"*Cel*, wake Ramona and send her to the infirmary, please. You needn't wake Carl."

"Aye, sir."

He carefully pulled the unconscious stranger from the pod and, cradling him like a baby, carried him to the Med-room where Ramona waited. "He needs oxygen. He ran out just before we recovered him. Let's hope we got him in time."

When the pod survivor finally revived, Neil asked him his name.

"John," he mumbled, "John Bauer," then he fell unconscious once again.

"Can you make some leeway with the man, Cel?" Neil said. "Got any trick?

She had one that John could neither prevent, nor frustrate. Resting a hand on his forehead, *Celestria's* avatar read his mind by analyzing what she understood about human gray matter.

He opened his eyes briefly, only to see Cel gently brushing errant hair from his eyes.

"You're safe, John," she said tenderly.

Although Celestria didn't probe too deeply, when next John came to, Neil had the answers he needed. "So, you're a Pastor?"

John studied the man who was casually dressed, but didn't answer.

"I'm Neil Avery, the captain of this craft."

"Oh, you … So this is where I meet my end, huh, butcher?"

Neil focused on the older man's eyes. "Wow, Pastor. News travels fast … and faster still when its wrong."

"Wrong? You going to tell me that you didn't destroy the *Princess*? Your picture was all over the cortex, Avery."

Ramona stepped next to Neil and smiled. "Relax, Pastor Bauer. You're among friends. How did you wind up way out here?"

John glanced at her but stayed focused on Neil. "I needn't answer your questions. You have my file, I presume. Why drag this out?"

Neil patted John's leg reassuringly through the blanket. "I neither have your file, Pastor Bauer, nor do I have any agenda beyond making a new friend. We found you adrift way out here and were wondering how that came to be."

John rolled his eyes and turned away.

Then Celestria stepped into his view and took his hand. "You needn't fear us, Pastor. You're not a prisoner. You'll have free reign of the ship as long as you're aboard her, and you'll soon come to know we mean you no harm."

Neil noted that of all the people in the room, John seemed transfixed by the ship's avatar. But even so, he refused to speak further.

"Well," Ramona said. "When you're feeling up to it, call for Celestria. Dinner is in a couple hours, and we'd love to have you."

Interlacing her arm with Neil's, Ramona coaxed him out of the room and down the corridor, passing Carl as they went.

"So," Carl said, "*Cel*, says we have a guest. How is he?"

"Suspicious," Neil said with out slowing.

"You of him, or he of us," Carl called after him.

"Yes," Neil answered without turning.

WHEN dinnertime rolled around, Neil and Ramona found themselves sitting alone.

"*Celestria*," Neil said, "any word about our guest?"

"He'll be along shortly, sir. Both he and Carl bring news."

"Oh, really?"

Ramona patted Neil's hand. "Patience, big boy. Enjoy the company you have."

Neil leaned on the table, fist to his cheek as he studied Ramona. "Well, how about that Slip-band drive, huh? Its transduction technology is something, isn't it? Boggles the mind," he teased.

Ramona rolled her eyes and glanced at the chronometer. "Where could they be?"

Neil chuckled. "Patience, girl. Enjoy the company you have."

Just then Carl came in followed by John, each taking a seat across from Neil and Ramona.

"Carl," Ramona said excitedly. "Your arm."

Carl raised the completely healed limb. "What? Is there something wrong?" Then he laughed and draped it over John's shoulders. "This guy, you've got to love him. He prayed for my arm and the pain melted away, just like that. And that's not the only thing Jesus healed. I've never felt more alive,"

"Best news ever!" she said jumping to her feet to look more closely.

"A miracle. I can't believe it," Neil said, as he followed her. "Is this even possible?"

"Apparently," Ramona said smugly, "there is a God after all. I think you can finally put away any doubts you may still have, flyboy."

This is incredible, thought Neil. If I hadn't seen it with my own eyes I'd … Hmm. He pinched Carl.

"Ouch! What was that for?"

"Sorry. Just had to make sure I wasn't dreaming."

"I think you were supposed to pinch your own arm," Carl scolded, rubbing where he'd just been assaulted. Carl gave Neil a stern look. "You'd think my wide-open eyes were a dead giveaway."

"I just had to test the reality, Carl. This seems so incredible."

Everyone sat, and, after prayer, dinner began.

"Carl caught me up on your stories, Neil. There's something I would like to discuss with all of you," John began. "I think I have something that might interest you. Have you ever heard of the Paladin project?"

Carl beamed. "You've got to hear this. It's a great system where those qualified are trained and financed by Providence to work inside the Coalition to change things from within."

Ramona raised a hand. "Wait a minute, please. Before we get into this discussion, I'd like to ask Pastor Bauer something."

"Yes, Miss French?"

"You see, sir, my name is the *something* I'd like to change. You can do wedding ceremonies, can't you?"

In surprise, Neil jumped to his feet. "Now wait just one moment."

Ramona stood and gathered his hands in hers. "Neil Douglas Avery, I love you. I have from the start. I want—"

"Stop." Neil pulled away and stepped back. "There's too much blood on my hands, woman. You deserve better."

"Does your reluctance, Neil, have anything to do with the *Emperor's Princess*?" John interrupted, "because there's something you should know about the liner. She carried Christians, sure, but that isn't why Dais had it shot down. It was a political move, pure and simple."

Both Neil and Ramona turned to give John their full attention.

"Proctor McCullough was aboard her as well."

"What?" Neil's face grew suddenly angry. "That bast—"

"Who?" Carl asked.

"Consul Dais' political rival," Neil growled. "Dais had *Wolverine* squad do his dirty work for him. I should have checked the manifest."

"You wouldn't have found McCullough on the ship's manifest, Neil," John said. "No one but the aristocracy knew until after the liner had been downed. Dais acted alone and without Senate sanction. He's been arrested for treason."

"Wow," Carl said, "this is big news."

"Bigger yet," John said, "McCullough was a pro-freedom Paladin; someone the proletariat has been aching to find. A dove, his political platform rested on the facts that this building threat of war was completely contrived by Dais and the Senate hawks, to wrest even more control from the people. He was already in the arena when he came to Christ. He and his political ideas were very appealing to the common voter and that threatened Dais' reign as High Consul. McCullough was killed for that, and that alone. No one knew of his affiliation with us."

Neil glanced at Ramona before focusing on John and Carl. "No matter what the political ramifications, I was still used to kill innocent people. What do you want me to do about that now?"

"Join the underground, Neil. As a Paladin you, Ramona, and Carl can make a difference."

Uncertain, Neil shook his head in reluctance.

Suddenly the room changed. He, Ramona, Carl, and John now stood in the white, never-ending room where Neil had faced Troy.

"What is this place? John said.

"This," Neil said, "is the heart of *Celestria*."

Wide-eyed, John looked around. "Rather big, isn't it?"

"I've never found its end."

Celestria's avatar stepped up to Neil. "There is nothing to distract you here, Capt. Avery, but you must understand that indecision and uncertainty are not your allies."

"Where do I go from here, Cel?"

"A prayer and a look into Heaven's mirror will help you find your way, sir."

Neil hesitated. Then, taking Ramona's hands in his, he drew her closer. In her eyes he found unwavering acceptance.

"John?"

"Yeah, Neil?"

"Perform weddings, do you?"

Chapter 22

Hope and Heartbreak

Five Years Later

RAMONA entered the bridge and slumped into the chair next to her husband.

Sitting at the helm, he turned to greet her. Rawboned and beardless, Neil Avery, tall and trim with an appealingly honest face, was still every inch a leader. He recognized her unease. "Too close to home, are we?"

She nodded faintly.

"Let's take a chance and see your folks," he said, putting his hand on her shoulder in gentle reassurance. "We're here."

Her heart leapt at the thought but quickly sank as reality gripped her. "It's too dangerous. The Consul has his troops on high-alert, and our presence might give my folks away, not to mention putting those in need of rescue in even more danger."

Turning fully to her, Neil took her hands; his strong fingers gave her a sense of safety, but his calm expression didn't fool her. His eyes said he was troubled by the prospect of explaining himself—*his history*—to her family just as much as she was.

Ramona slid to the chair's edge, leaned forward, and pulled Neil's hands around her expanded waist—*the baby due any day*—then embraced his neck to whisper in his ear. "I love you. You and I are not the same people we were back then. We're a family now. We've got one child and another one on the way. We have to consider their safety."

"Safety? We'll be careful. Your folks should meet their grandchildren."

"I want to see my folks. You know I do, but there are heavy emotional issues that will take time to work through."

"We've had five years."

"But they haven't. My folks don't even know I'm alive."

"But Honey, you *are* alive, and they must be told. There's no way to ease them into any of this information, but they should know we're married, and that they are grandparents."

"I know, and as important as those things are, Neil, that's not the main issue. We are not the same people that we were back then."

"Sure. Because of time, ... and God."

Ramona dropped her gaze. "And *Celestria*, and what she did to us."

Neil lifted her chin to meet him eye to eye. "Ramona, that's not what's holding you back. Your fear goes beyond explaining *Celestria* to them. What's wrong?"

"I know you, Neil. You won't let your past stay in the past. Before we meet my folks, you need to settle this *Emperor's Princess* thing in your own heart. You are not to blame."

"How could I not be to blame? I led the mission. I flew the lead Dart. I released the torpedo that sent the *Princess* careening into the atmosphere. Even so …" Neil tightened his grip on her hands. "… your family deserves to be told you didn't die."

She watched his lips thin in displeasure at the situation that kept them at odds, but he kept his voice even. "When things settle down, somewhere along the line, we have to see your folks."

"I've made up my mind that a meeting with my parents isn't going to happen, at least not anytime soon. Back to business. We have a mission to think of."

Neil kissed her cheek and pushed away.

Ramona knew where he was coming from. He hadn't always been an honorable man, but he was trying, and he had made progress. He didn't swagger anymore, mentally or physically. But he was a man not yet at peace with himself, his history; less so when facing anyone who might know his past. Problem was, he hadn't yet tapped into a strength greater than his own. For five years she had tried to get him to understand the concept of God's forgiveness, but it hadn't sunk in. He still needed …

"You know what?" he said, "You're right. We're on a rescue mission, and we don't need to be distracted right now. The Enforcers are out on a tear. The underground church is at risk."

She sighed and turned away to get ready.

Neil caught her arm and turned her. "Don't you ever step from this ship thinking you're not my world. I love you." He drew her close to hold her tight.

Yes! she thought. We need this.

"Hmm," she cooed with a broad smile. "I could stay in your arms forever."

"If only people weren't waiting to be rescued." Clearly reluctant to let her go, he held her in his strong arms and tenderly kissed her.

Just then, *Celestria* touched down and relaxed into place … on Atheron. It was time to go.

Chapter 23
Hope and Tears

RAMONA AVERY entered the alley. Two families, she told herself, just two families three little blocks away then it's back to the ship. Glad their homes are close.

Her condition wasn't going to make her assignment easy. She ran a gentle hand over her enlarged belly, quieting the baby, and looked back to see her spaceship hidden amid the trees of the schoolyard. That meager covering and dusk, weren't much, but it was all they had until *Celestria's* energy stores were recharged.

If not for the fact that there were too many people to fetch and too few people to do the fetching, Mona wouldn't have participated in this rescue at all. She really didn't like putting the baby in danger, but there simply was no other way. What if she went into labor when she was away from the ship? The thought of that possibility grumbled in the back of her mind.

This run shouldn't take long, but her maternity dress, though comfortable, wasn't her preferred outfit for a rescue. She shook herself, and took a deep breath. Focus, girl, focus, she thought, straightening herself to concentrate on her assigned task. Alert to danger, she scanned the alley ahead, her fanny pack bouncing lightly on her hip as she walked.

If things went as planned, she could make it

to the first house well before Spirita arose. If not, the giant gas planet would remove the cover of night, leaving her and the others exposed to hostile eyes.

As she neared the Barretts' house, the unmistakable sounds of glass breaking and objects being slammed against walls said Coalition Enforcers had arrived ahead of her. She peeked through a bedroom window.

A green clad soldier had tossed drawers and their contents everywhere and was now yanking clothes from the closet to search it also.

Blasted Enforcers, she thought. Just once couldn't things go smoothly?

She crept to the open dining room window and hunkered down below it. Hidden from the street by a large bush, she slipped her TCP (Tactical Communications Pod) from the fanny pack. Careful to hide its screen's glow with a cupped hand, she read the yellow-lettered text. … Edward, Margery, and Jacob Barrett.

From the TCP, Mona launched a micro-fly and guided the tiny airborne camera into the room to rest where it could give her a clear view of everyone and everything.

Crouched behind the bush, she assessed the situation. Ed Barrett sat at the table with his son, Jacob. Mona saw abject fear in his eyes. Surely, as a Christian, Ed knew this day was a possibility, but even a calm, difficult to provoke man would have been unnerved at the sight of a Mouser M-1-AH Hand-cannon aimed squarely at his teenage boy. Dinner, interrupted by the soldiers, was on the table, but no one had eaten.

Although Margery, Ed's wife, was behind and to one side of the officer, out of his line of sight, she was openly breaking the law. Her hands were raised heavenward, and her lips moving. There was no worse time to openly pray. If the Enforcer or either of his men saw her doing that, she was dead—she and her family.

Mona touched her TCP's screen, switching it to her husband's image, which swaying and jostling as he walked, his voice clear in her earpiece. "Yeah, hon. What's up?"

"Neil," she whispered. "Enforcers have the Barretts. I can't get past their house to the Oberlys without being seen.

"How many Enforcers?"

"Three."

"I shouldn't have put you and the baby at risk, Ramona. Three Enforcers against you alone? I can't have that. Abort the mission."

"Hon, I … I …"

In the frame of her TCP, she could see Neil had stopped walking to talk. "Honey, they found Henderson's Bible, and shot him and his wife."

Ramona gasped and glanced away. When she looked back, she could barely see the screen through her tears but pushed aside her anger to speak. "I'm not leaving. I'll not let these idiots have the Barretts without a fight." She pulled a gun from her fanny pack.

169

"Ramona, there's no one to back you up. Get back to the ship."

She raised her pistol to check the setting. "I'll be careful, Neil. As always, baby comes first, but I'll wait out the Enforcers and hope they don't find anything incriminating."

"No, hon. I want you to—"

She cut him off and switched to the microfly's view of the Barretts and zoomed in. Her intention was to protect Jacob first, then Margery if it should come to that. Gripping her gun, she considered a shootout with the soldiers. Only as a last resort, she told herself.

"Lord," Ramona whispered, "please answer Margery. Give her a reason to drop her hands."

Of the Barretts, Jacob had the greatest need. The Enforcer's standard issue rifle, a weapon without a *stun* setting, was leveled squarely at the teen's forehead. But that didn't make sense. Why target the boy and not his father who sat near him? What kind of a threat did the kid pose? Was the gangly fifteen-year-old the greater risk to the officer and his men? Nevertheless the gun didn't waiver.

Blood-gang! Mona gasped. Revenge-minded teens—vicious sewer rats banding together—now posed the principal danger to Enforcers in cities everywhere; even to these heavily armed troopers despite their traveling in three-man strike teams like these men. Could this young kid really be a blood-gang member?

"You're right, Dad," Jacob said. "Enforcers

170

are cool. Is that a real Mouser M-1-AH Hand-cannon, mister?"

What? Ramona's focus narrowed on the confusing teenager. He sounds as if he *wants* to be an Enforcer. Was that the reason Mom was praying? Her son *wants* to be an Enforcer?

Ed's voice quivered. "I'm tellin' ya, boy, that's the job to have when you grow up. Being an Enforcer has every advantage."

Without turning his head, the squad leader glanced sideways at Ed Barrett and then shifted his eyes back toward Jacob who carried an innocent, admiring smile.

In light of what the soldiers were doing to his home, Jacob's attitude seemed bizarre. But it was better that the officer kept his eyes on the boy and his dad than to turn and see Margery praying.

Maybe Mona could end this sooner than not. Her gun could rapid-fire, and her aim was impeccable. If the soldiers didn't leave soon, she'd have to take matters into her own hands anyway. Spirita's appearance was growing ever closer; the distant horizon was already showing signs of her arrival.

Two Enforcers were accounted for, and she hoped the other was doing his part to trash the third room. Better *that* than he sneak up behind her. An icy chill ran up her spine. *She turned with a start.* Nothing. Relieved, she refocused on the crisp, forest green uniformed leader.

He turned fully toward Ed Barrett, then,

171

almost robotically, his head pivoted once again toward Jacob, and his eyes narrowed. Did he see some flaw in the boy's expression; a chink or crack revealing Jacob's true feelings? Or was the boy serious about his wanting to become an Enforcer?

Ready to strike, Ramona raised her gun. Patience, she thought. Let this play out. I still have a little time yet.

The Enforcer's voice was ice, his eyes full of hate. "*You* want to be an Enforcer, boy?"

Despite his obvious fear, Jacob answered the Enforcer as if he had just been recruited.

"Yes, Sir! In a couple years I'll enlist for sure." Ignoring the ruckus in the other rooms, Jacob smiled even more.

Well, that's not what I expected. Ramona thought tersely. Everything about the cold-blooded snake in human flesh made her blood boil, including his choice of weapon.

She checked her gun again. Yeah, yeah, it's fully charged. Keep a cool head, girl.

If she was slow on the draw, one electro-charged bullet from his hand cannon would rip a grapefruit-sized hole clean through her chest.

That would go over swell for the baby, wouldn't it? She pushed the thought out of her head, but the sounds of smashed glass and breaking wood were starting to get to her, *that,* and *Margery's* reaction to it all. Mrs. Barrett winced at every sound, but neither opened her eyes nor lowered her hands.

They would have little left when the soldiers were finished, *that is,* if the Barretts were to survive this ordeal at all. Come on, Margery, drop your arms and open your eyes already. Being quiet isn't going to keep his attention off you forever.

The captain took a step toward Edward, leaning to get right in his face. "You okay with that, Barrett, your boy being an Enforcer?"

Ramona thought she could smell the soldier's garlicky breath from where she crouched. Hang tough, Eddy. Protect your family.

With a trembling voice, Ed forced a smile. "Good gravy, sir, who wouldn't be? I tried to enlist, myself, but I washed out. You guys are tough, and only the best of the best make it. I'd be proud to see my son do what I couldn't."

Ramona frowned. How could he not get in? With his broad beefy shoulders and burly arms, Ed was no small man. He must be playing with the Enforcer's oversized ego to keep his attention off Margery. There was no other explanation.

The Enforcer cocked his head. "Well, you're a big enough man, that's for sure. Perhaps you lack the brains."

Don't bite, Ed. Let it go. Middle of the twenty-third century, and civility still eludes these idiot Enforcers. Just let it go.

Ed took a nervous breath. "Actually, I got high marks in school. I'm smart but …"

The officer's nostrils flared. He pressed his rifle barrel into Ed's cheek. "But what?" His voice, though soft, was cold with threat.

Ramona perked up. But what? But you had no desire to be a jerk with a gun, like him? But the Coalition stinks to high heaven? Lot's of catch phrases to hang on that nail, Eddy. Pick a good one.

Mr. Barrett took another labored breath and diverted his eyes. "But I lacked the nerve. You guys are tough, and I'm … well …"

The officer lowered his gun, apparently satisfied no insult was forthcoming.

Ed looked at his son, grabbed his hand, and gave it a firm squeeze before turning back to the officer. Although quaking, his voice was filled with pride.

"I hope Jacob can get into the academy. He studies hard and gets better grades than I did. He has a steady heart, too. Being an Enforcer one day is all he talks about. You can value those qualities in my boy, can't you?"

Not believing the officer would buy the load of swill he was being served, Ramona held her breath as she clutched her gun. Her muscles tightened as she prepared to jump to her feet, spin, and fire.

On the TCP she saw something else in Barrett's gaze though, the way he looked at his son, and Jacob was in on it, as well. You're tag teaming the Enforcer, aren't you? With his attention on either one of you, he won't notice

Margery praying.

But Ramona noticed, and with a sweaty palm, squeezed her pistol grip tighter. Would Margery ever end her prayer? If she didn't quit soon, they would be discovered, and that would be the end of them. Margery was putting everyone at risk by praying openly. What was the point?

The officer glanced around the table. "Oh, did we interrupt your supper? Pretty fancy fixin's for the middle of the week, isn't it?"

Mona's jaw tightened. Roast beef with all the trimmings, a luxury, loudly said that the Barretts planned to leave Atheron this midweek night. Last supper here, is it? Couldn't just let a good hunk of meat go to waste, huh, Marge? The Enforcer had them cold.

But before the officer turned her way, Mrs. Barrett opened her eyes and lowered her arms to rest a friendly hand on the man's shoulder. "Jacob has just decided to join the academy, sir. We have much to celebrate and would be honored if you fine gentlemen joined us."

What? Ramona thought. We don't have time for this!

The officer glanced back at the table. Although the roast was still steaming hot, with its delicately seasoned fragrance filling the room and stealing into the alley, his reply, "Huh!" said he'd rather take a hammer to his own foot. But the inherent strength in Mrs. Barrett's smile didn't lessen.

As young Jacob timidly raised his hand, Ramona held her breath. Oh, no. Now what? She checked the horizon, the outlying hills; Spirita hadn't crested yet, but time was really getting short.

Satisfied the mom was harmless, the officer turned back toward Jacob and scowled. "What do you want, boy?"

Jacob's admiration beamed even more. "Can I get your autograph on something, sir?"

The officer measured Jacob's expression. His reply was matter-of-fact, like Jacob's request was common. "Sure."

Give me a break. As if …, thought Ramona.

The boy got up and rushed over to the shards of broken door trim strewn across his living room floor—evidence of an Enforcer's typical method of entry—and picked up a good-sized piece. Blue paint covered its face and one edge, but on the backside the bare wood was smooth enough to write on.

"Wow. My friends will not believe this."

The Enforcer shouldered his Mouser and took a pen from his pocket.

"Could you sign it 'To my friend, Jacob?' You know, to make my buds jealous."

The officer handed the shard back to Jacob and called to his men, "There's nothing here. Let's go!" Then he looked back at the boy. "You bring that piece of wood with you when you're ready to enlist, and I'll get you in."

"Thanks, man. Thanks a lot." Jake followed

him and his two men to the door and stared after them as they walked up the street.

Hmm, well played, Ramona thought.

From behind the bush, she peered out to make a mental note of the Enforcer's face. Should she and he ever meet again, it would be his turn to be on the business end of the gun.

The Enforcer looked back to see young Jacob standing on the doorsill, waving the autographed shard high over his head.

The officer raised his rifle and shook it as if to say, "Power to the Coalition." Then, wearing a malicious smile, he kicked in their neighbor's door. The Barrett's door had not been locked, and Mona doubted old man Oberly's was either.

Point taken.

"You did well, son." Ed's voice was now noticeably calm.

As the boy stepped back into his house, Ramona quietly came around to the front of the building and saw him toss the piece of wood into the trashcan. Apparently the kid wanted little to do with being an Enforcer. Sweet play-acting, youngster.

Ed patted Jacob's back. "Like a pro, son. You hid your dislike, *and* kept your head."

She realized that Ed, indeed, had been faking his nervousness. Ramona felt she couldn't have done better herself.

But once the Enforcers were gone, Jacob looked as though he wanted to vomit, not so much as meeting his father's gaze.

Ramona peeked deeper in to catch Ed's concerned expression for his son, and decided to give them a moment together while she hurried next door to the Oberly's house.

Stealthily, she peered though a window.

Mr. Oberly was a pretty wise man. That he and the Mrs. had an open Bible laid out for all to see came as quite a shock. The old man seemed to sense her presence at the window because he made a subtle motion with his hand for her to leave them to their fate.

The hope of eternal peace outweighed the old couple's physical safety; she saw *that* written in the old man's face. With what was sure to follow, she knew better than to stick around and watch.

Disquieted by a heart mixed with hope and tears, Ramona went back to the Barrett's house, all the while praying for the old couple. In this war, everyone had his orders. Apparently Mr. and Mrs. Oberly were to be bold and take a stand. Maybe they'd gain new ground for God's glory. Maybe—*maybe not*—but there was always hope.

Chapter 24

The Rescue

THE mess the Enforcers made was daunting, but Jacob stooped anyway to pick up the broken bits of doorjamb scattered across the floor.

Hurried footsteps padded behind him, and he turned with a start. A strange woman rushed into their house and drew a blind over the window that looked toward the Oberlys. She glanced at Jacob, then at his folks, and asked if they were packed and ready.

What! What was she talking about?

As the woman went to the open door to look toward the neighbor's house, Jake saw she was far into her pregnancy. In spite of it, her face mesmerized him as her long raven curls, caught by the breeze, caressed her cheek.

Then he saw the gun.

What a study in contrasts! Pistol held high, *pregnant,* drop dead gorgeous, the lady was nothing less than extraordinary any way you looked at it.

Who was she? Coalition citizens couldn't possess weapons and, by her expression, Jake knew he needn't point out she was breaking the law. When she looked at him again, the seriousness in her eyes snapped him back to reality. Their situation was grave, and Jake had better get a grip. He diverted his eyes.

"Are you Jacob?" Her soft, assured tone was calming despite the stressful situation.

"Yes, ma'am. My friends call me Jake."

"I'm Captain Star, Jake. Remember this, will you? When you're right where God wants you, you're bulletproof."

"Captain Star?"

"Yeah, Jake?"

"Then why the gun?"

At the sound of breaking glass, she turned toward the neighbor's house. "Because the bad guys—*they* aren't."

"They aren't what, where God wants them, or bulletproof?"

"One in the same, isn't it?" she said before turning to Jake's dad to nod.

His dad pulled suitcases from behind the couch and, with one in each hand, brushed past them and headed out.

His mom nudged Jake toward the door, but when he remembered her mealtime efforts, he held back to glance at the table: *roast beef, mashed potatoes, gravy, green beans, and biscuits*. Her best, but a knot in his gut had replaced his appetite.

Captain Star craned her neck to see what held his attention. "They invite themselves to dinner, but Enforcers never appreciate what you offer or your hard work. Lousy guests, huh?"

Jake half nodded as his mom pressed him forward and through the doorway.

A moment later, the petite gun bearer

followed them out.

Ahead of them, his daddy hurried around the corner and down the dark alley. The sun had set, but by the light of the Dalvus nebula, Jake could still make out enough to get by. It would be nearly as bright as day when Spirita rose; he figured that was why they hurried. His head swam with questions and confusion, but this wasn't the time or place to demand answers.

The next moment, Jake thought he heard a blaster pop off a couple of rounds.

His mother stopped short to look across the backyard fences. "Oh, my!" she said under her breath. Concern for their neighbors' safety was written all over her face.

Dad didn't stop. Jake didn't want to stop either but, like his mom, he had to look. Was it the Oberlys' house or the one beyond?

Captain Star caught and clutched the arms of Jake and his mother to press them forward. "Don't stop! Keep going!"

Jake could hear his dad huff and puff as he hurried down the alley. The canvas suitcases, filled to the max, bulged at the seams.

His dad glanced back from time to time to see if the others kept up.

Jacob hurried to his side to take a suitcase, which nearly yanked his arm off as soon as he caught the full weight of it. What's this thing filled with, he thought, Mom's cast iron skillets? Well, now I know why Dad's struggling.

As Captain Star caught up to Jake, movement behind a fence caught his eye. A whimpering mutt watched them but otherwise sat quietly. Next, they passed a Doberman, but it didn't so much as snarl.

"Would you look at that?" Jake said to the Captain as his mom padded up behind them.

"Evidence, Mr. Barrett. It's evidence," Captain Star said. Clearly distracted, she kept glancing over her shoulder.

"Evidence of what?"

"Of *whom*, Jacob. Evidence of *whom*. Keep your eyes open. There *will* be more."

Jake glanced back. "But dogs normally bark at the slightest sound. What's with this?"

His mom patted his shoulder to set his mind at rest. "You'll understand in time, son. Just praise God they're silent tonight."

Jacob tried not to stare as he looked at Captain Star's weapon; although it was small, it seemed mean enough. "You ever kill anyone?"

"Jacob!"

His mom was right. The moment the words left his mouth he felt bad about it.

"Sorry, ma'am."

Alert to any possible danger, Captain Star glanced back over her shoulder once more before tucking her pistol away. But she stayed by his side and whispered, "I've seen my share of firefights, Jake. Been in one or two. It's a dangerous place, this universe of ours."

"Yes, this 'verse is a dangerous place, but that didn't answer my question."

"And you see this alley as the place to press the issue?"

Despite her answer, he liked her. He liked the sound of her voice, and he liked the way she talked to him. Conversing with her as an equal made him feel like an adult.

"I think my teacher suspected I was a Christian. If someone called the cops on us, it would have been her."

"That seems like a stretch, Jake. So what happened? Did she see you treat someone with respect and take note?"

"Then why are we on the run?"

She shrugged. "Things happen."

After crossing a few side streets, they arrived at Hedrick High. In the schoolyard, to Jake's surprise, sat an old space-freighter.

On its rear were traces of its name, "*Dangerous Haul*," or some such thing. Years of neglect had worn some of the letters faint.

Spirita had risen high enough to reflect the sun's light. The magnificent gas giant exposed their escape. Out of time and out of options, Jake's parents ran for the ship, but Jake noticed Captain Star—*Mrs. Past-due*—struggled to keep pace, so he held back.

He recognized others from his church nearer the ship. Pastor hurried toward them from another direction, followed by other families.

As the gathering people lined up at the ramp, Captain Star waited off to one side, maybe to catch her breath, Jake thought, ... or

… she wouldn't be going into labor, would she?

Her behavior seemed very strange, almost trance-like. She slowly drew the gun from her fanny pack.

What is she doing? he asked himself.

· Jake's pastor called out and pointed to an Enforcer coming their way.

He sees us, Jake thought.

The officer shouted and started running toward the ship.

Captain Star turned, took careful aim, and fired. The officer flew backward and crashed to the ground in a heap.

Jacob's stomach clenched as if he, too, had been hit. He had never seen a man die before, hoped he never would, but he knew what Zithion-charged bullets could do to flesh. He had seen it demonstrated on a side of beef once. Sickened, he jerked away.

Startled, the folks ahead of Jake clamored up the ramp and into the ship. A man, and the families he led, came running down the street from a different direction. His followers scrambled up the ramp, but he stopped, put his hands on his hips and frowned at the Barrett's lady escort as if she'd done something wrong. Was it about the guy she shot, or something else?

Jake entered the ship, found a seat, and peered out at Captain Star as she fell into the man's arms.

He kissed her forehead, and then they

hurried up the ramp.

Her smile, though faint, seemed out of place in contrast to the officer there on the ground, unmoving.

Jacob felt disgusted by Captain Star's callused action. Catching her arm as they passed by, he stopped her, hardly able to get the words out. "Ma'am, why'd you kill that man?"

Why did he ask when he knew the answer? Given half a chance, he would have done the same, but didn't believe he would have enjoyed it as much as she seemed to. Or worse, maybe he would have enjoyed it more.

Letting the man go on without her, she eased onto the cushioned bench and placed a gentle hand on Jake's shoulder. Her dark brown eyes bore deep concern, her voice, compassion.

"In a war, people die, Mr. Barrett. None of us enjoy taking life, but sometimes, to save others or yourself, you must. However, when we can …" She tapped the glass and pointed to the man on the ground. "Watch."

Right then the officer's body jerked back to life. Struggling to his feet, and teetering like a drunk, he staggered toward the ship just as it sealed up.

She smiled and spoke without taking her eyes from the Enforcer. "… electro-charged rubber bullets. He's okay, but he'll have a nasty, prickly feeling in every fiber of his body for the next few hours. Knowing *that* brings a smile to my face." She cocked her head and winked at the boy next to her. "Call me mean, Jake, but that's less than he deserves, don't you think?"

Simple truth was, given that the officer was a heartless, murdering Enforcer, Jake had to agree. He fantasized about taking revenge himself for all the hardship aimed at him over the years.

Even as the ship lifted off, he felt a tug from Atheron. A desire to go back and set the score straight wouldn't let go.

"Where are we heading?"

The smile in her eyes glinted with hope. "Away from here," she said, adding no more.

Jake believed the Oberlys met the same end assigned every Christian discovered by the Coalition. "Captain Star, I don't see hiding or running away as fighting back. The Enforcers should've been stopped before they ..." Jake looked away.

A gentle finger under his chin, Captain Star turned his head so he'd meet her eye to eye. "Sam and Clara Oberly?"

Holding back a flood of emotion, he shrugged halfheartedly. "If *I* had a gun ..."

"There are ways to overcome the enemy without shedding blood."

"Yeah, well," he mumbled, "drawing blood is all they understand."

"Perhaps. But we Christians aren't them."

He turned his attention to the city lights beyond the window. "I can't help it. I want to settle the score."

She ran gentle fingers through his hair. "I understand what you're saying, Jacob. But there are other ways—*constructive ways*—to settle the score."

What made her an expert on how to settle things? Even though she had an answer to everything, he couldn't get a handle on her. But she had just saved his family's lives. That in itself needed some show of appreciation.

"Ma'am?"

"Yeah, hon?"

"Thank you for rescuing us."

When she smiled and winked at him, in spite of himself, his spirits rose, almost matching the upward thrust of their craft.

Her right brow arched slightly, as if to disclose a secret. "You will rescue me one day, mighty man of God."

By all accounts, it was a big 'verse, so the odds against his ever meeting her again were beyond numbers, weren't they? To see himself one day rescuing her was just absurd. Jake studied her dark eyes. Even while pregnant, she seemed able to face any obstacle and deal with it handily, but how could she know what the future held when she couldn't see what was right in front of her? He was no man of God. But then, that was his secret, wasn't it?

Nearly halfway across town, he spotted his house growing smaller by the millisecond and pointed it out to change the subject. "I hope Mom turned off the oven."

She chuckled. "And that matters?" Then, as the ship crested the next hill, Jake saw her expression change.

Nestled in the next valley was the hulking remains of the *Emperor's Princess*. Overgrown with weed and vine, the onetime luxury liner was no more than the ship's midsection lying on its side.

Beyond it were the Seychelles village lights. Captain Star rested her fingers on the window as though she were touching the village or someone she loved there, and as she stared, her lower lip began to quiver and tears filled her eyes. Abruptly, without a word, she rose and hurried past the other passengers to another part of the ship.

He wanted to stop her and ask about her tie to Seychelles, but he didn't know what to say.

He stared back out at the ship's ruins. Maybe *that* was the connection. Maybe Captain Star had reasons for revenge all her own. Perhaps one day he would learn who his rescuer really was and discover her relationship to the *Emperor's Princess* or Seychelles. Then again, maybe not. It *was* a big universe after all, and Atheron certainly didn't account for much of it.

He watched the ground fade as they rocketed up and away, and got a sense that the future held far more than he might imagine.

Chapter 25

The Answer

PASTOR JOHN BAUER peeked into the bridge.

Ramona pulled back from Neil's embrace, turning away to wipe moisture from her cheeks.

Neil beckoned. "Come in, John."

John hesitated before stepping through the threshold. "Look, I can come back later."

"No, come in. You need something?"

"Just to report that everyone's settled in. The next few weeks will be rough, but I think our passengers will handle camping in the cargo bay well enough." John stepped fully into the room. "Are you okay, Mona?"

She turned, forced a smile, and with a quick jerk of the head, beckoned to him. "Just a little too close to home, John. This place has brought back old memories, and I just let hormones get the better of me. I suppose I'm just being silly."

"To rescue the Barretts, you not only fought against the hormones of your pregnancy but against a strong natural urge to protect the baby as well. At any moment you could make Neil a two-time daddy, and yet you succeeded in the rescue." John came closer to pat her shoulder. "It was risky going out as you did, Mona. You were very brave."

"She was foolish," Neil scolded, but Mona ignored the comment.

"Would you join us at Captain's mess,

John?" she said, changing the subject.

"*Celestria's* cooking? Sure, Mona, I'm always up for—"

"Tonight, supper is on me, John. *Cel* will be serving our passengers."

"Sounds even better. I love your cooking, Mona." Trying to reserve his true reasons for being there, John took the second's seat, but turned to face his hosts.

"Three hundred souls rescued this day."

Neil took the pilot's seat and turned toward the pastor. "I'm sorry, John. I wish we could have done more."

John shrugged and shook his head once. "From the start, Neil, I knew we couldn't save everyone. But we did better than I thought. Neither of you should think otherwise."

"Enforcers were everywhere. Still, I hate to think we left anyone behind."

"Those that couldn't make it to the ship were instructed to go to the underground churches in Hastings and Baldwin. From there they'll be funneled to the outlying villages. God is with them. Believe that."

Mona took a seat next to John to hold his hand. "I barely made it away with the Barretts. I had to leave—"

"Clara and Sam Oberly. Yeah, I know. You didn't really have a choice." John wrapped a comforting arm around her shoulders. "I didn't want to think about it, but I knew Sam would want to stay. The old geezer ached to save souls, he and Clara both. Their second wish was to go quickly when their time came. They were ready. Chuck Henderson was the same way. I doubt his Bible being found was an accident."

Mona studied John's face.

John shot a quick, questioning look at Neil before turning back to her. "Look, there's something else I need to discuss with you two."

Attentive, Neil leaned forward. "Come on, buddy, we're listening."

John mindlessly stared at nothing to collect his thoughts. "I've known you two for, what has been, five years now?"

"Yeah?" Neil said. "Is there a problem?"

John pulled a picture from his pocket, considered it, and then handed it to Mona.

"Hmm, a photo of us, Neil. A wedding picture." She handed it to her husband.

Staring at the photo, Neil got to his feet. "What're you saying, John? You weren't legally able to marry us? All this time, Mona and I—"

"No, no, no, nothing like that." John stood and tapped the picture. "Look at it, will you? Neither of you have aged a day in five years."

With blank eyes, Neil looked up at John. "You've *got* to be kidding."

John felt his brow tighten. Maybe Neil was right. Maybe John was just being silly. Five years doesn't age a soul much, but Neil was now thirty and Mona twenty-six. No. No, each should look his or her age but neither did; neither came close.

He tapped the picture again. "What will people say in five ... ten years down the road when your youth becomes too obvious to hide? How will you respond then?"

Wearing a salient smile, Neil shoved the picture back into John's hand. "You know ... I wonder what Terisa is up to? Seems high time I checked on my little girl." Neil called for the door to Terisa's room, and saying no more, stepped through when it dilated open.

John called out, but his words came too late. Neil was gone. The iris closed leaving nothing behind but a smooth, bare wall. John stared at it for a brief moment before giving Mona his attention. "Why the secrecy?"

"John," Mona said. "I wanted to talk to you about Jake Barrett. I know he's only fifteen, but I'd like to recommend him to the Paladin Academy. Do you think his parents would—"

"What are you two hiding, Mona?"

"Hiding?" Mona knit her brow as if John's suspicions were a non-issue. "John, can I speak to you about Jacob for a moment?"

"I'll speak to his folks, Mona. Okay? But why are you two being so ... so ... evasive? Sometimes trying to get an answer from either of you is exasperating!" He threw up his hands and turned away.

He heard Mona turn her chair behind him. "I suppose you want the whole story then? Very well, if you insist. *Celestria*, to the bridge, please."

Appearing from nowhere the ship's avatar moved to Mona's side, looking almost as human as anyone, but somehow less so ... or *more* so

… depending on one's tastes. With her fair features, perfect skin, and golden hair, the holographicly constructed humanoid avatar was beyond beautiful.

"Yes, Captain Avery?" Celestria's voice was soft, feminine, and almost musical.

John shook himself. Despite his best efforts to appear unimpressed, the avatar always stole his breath away.

Without taking her eyes off John, Mona spoke to Celestria. "Pastor John would like to know our story. Could you take a moment to catch him up?"

"As you wish, Captain Avery. What time frame do you want me to project?"

"Start with our escape from Atheron and end where we find Pastor Bauer adrift."

"Aye, Captain." Celestria turned to face John. "Ready?" She reached to touch his forehead but John held her hand at bay.

"Is this going to hurt?" he said.

"Pastor, you should be careful for what you ask." Celestria smiled and pushed past his hand to touch his brow.

At once the tavern flashed through John's mind, instantly seeing Ramona through Neil's eyes and him through hers as their emotions regarding each other clashed in a tumultuous mix of hate, rage, adulation and … secret desire.

Images, sensations, fragrances, emotions, and thoughts—disjointed and mixed—covering months overpowered him.

John Bauer reared away from *Celestria's*

hand, staggered back, and stumbled into a chair.

Cocking her head, Celestria regarded him with concern as she lowered her hand.

"The images may confuse you, Pastor Bauer, until your mind sorts through them, but I think you'll adjust."

He shook his head. "Easy for you to say! My head's a scrambled mess. What was that?"

"You have the memories of Captains Neil and Ramona, as well as mine from the time starting at the Tavern, to your rescue from the life pod. I also gave you a portion of Carlton Ogier's memories so that you would fully understand the Averys' circumstances."

Celestria turned toward Mona. "Will that be all, ma'am?"

Ramona nodded but said nothing.

Celestria vanished.

Awkward with the baby, Mona struggled to get up from the Captain's chair.

"John, I trust you'll keep our secrets?"

He nodded. "Yeah, once I understand them, sure. How long did this process take? How long was I out?"

"Only a moment. Celestria had just touched you."

John shook himself. "I've got days ... no, weeks of memories of you three ... and a headache to match."

"Us four, John," Ramona clarified. "You forget *Celestria*."

John feigned a smile. "I hardly consider *Celestria* a person."

Ramona raised an eyebrow. "Oh, really? Wasn't Celestria the first person you responded to after we rescued you? Thought you saw an angel, you said."

"Yeah, well … I was deprived of oxygen. Makes a man see things that aren't really there."

"Come on now. Ever since you discovered she was our ship's projected personality you've treated her poorly."

"I just hate being fooled, Mona." John remembered the first time he saw Celestria's angelic face. Her eyes, a profound sapphire blue, although filled with concern, had an unnatural shimmer in them. She had gently brushed away errant hair from his forehead, and said, "You're safe now. I'll keep you safe."

"When I discovered she wasn't heaven sent, it kind of took the wind from my sails, you know? I thought at seeing her, Jesus would soon follow. Oh, well."

"So *Celestria*, her avatar anyway, makes you long for your eternal reward?"

"I beg your pardon?" John said. "Oh, no, no." he said as he caught her meaning. "I'm not thinking about leaving yet. I just felt cheated by your machine, is all."

"Oh, stop. You're fooling no one, John. From the start, we knew you didn't know what to make of her. You're a good man, but you can't expect to hide your unease by treating our companion with so little respect. You just need to come to grips about what you feel about her. And for goodness sake, treat her like the good person she is."

"I meant no offence—"

Ramona chuckled. "Yes, you did."

"Yes, I did." John diverted his eyes. "I guess I was just pushing back against my confusion. In the back of my head I probably still see her as an angel, and so, to fight that …"

"She's not an angel, John. When you finally admit that the holographic representation of our ship touched some deep pocket in your emotions, your attitude will change. You need to lighten up."

"Was I *that* transparent?"

Ramona's smile said she believed so.

"I'm sorry for my uncalled-for rudeness, *Celestria*. I apologize. Will you forgive me?"

The avatar appeared, considered John briefly, and then stepped forward to hug him.

Still awkward and unsure of himself, John held her ineptly and then pulled back, glancing about in an effort to hide his renewed unease.

The avatar smiled. "Your apology is accepted, Pastor Bauer. And now that *that* is out of the way, sir, perhaps you can focus your thoughts on Captain Neil?" And with that, she once again vanished.

John shut his eyes and gave a deep sigh. "These memories … I see now what Neil has been through. Always in the back of his mind, the *Princess* stands as a wall Neil can't see a way past. To him, it symbolizes his entire past. He desperately needs to get beyond it and put it behind him once and for all."

He rubbed his brow. The painful throb of the massive information download was nonstop.

"John, what you see in your mind's eye, and the emotions you feel, belong to the Neil of five years ago. The anguish you sense is even worse for him today. I sleep with the man, and I can tell you there are nights when he awakens in sweat and tears. I feel so helpless."

John met her gaze with understanding. *Celestria's* memory download was starting to arrange itself in a coherent manner. The pain Neil bore was only now starting to make sense.

"For both of you; the gene modification has brought you back to a pre-Noah state of being, hasn't it? This one hundred twenty year cap God has placed on man's lifespan no longer applies to you, does it?"

"No, John. It doesn't." Ramona's answer was matter-of-fact. There was simply no other way to put it.

"So, not only does Neil's guilt grow, but knowing he has an extended lifespan makes it even worse for him, doesn't it?"

Although Mona held her posture straight and noble, and despite her self-confident smile, a single tear trailing down her cheek betrayed her distress. Neil's pain was her pain, and its intensity was no longer hidden from John. The two sat in silence for a long moment.

"John," Wanting to get this right, Ramona hesitated to collect her thoughts. "… on the day we first found your life-pod adrift and brought you aboard, we left you in the infirmary to recover. You rewarded Carl's soon to follow visit with a prayer of healing."

"Yeah?"

"Could that happen again?" Mona turned away and paced two steps to choose her words carefully and then turned back to him. "Now that you understand Neil's anguish, can you pray for him as you did for Carl?"

John stood, came to her, and gathered her hands in his. "I wish it were that simple, Mona. I really do. But the root of Neil's torment is his unbelief in God. God has forgiven him, but until he receives it and believes it's true, he'll carry his anguish always."

John now knew that from the beginning of the genetic transfer Ramona understood and felt Neil's remorse, but she also grasped what Neil had failed to realize about himself; that God had forgiven him.

John understood the depth to which she was drawn to Neil. A nurturer by nature, coupled with what Mona had learned of Neil, to see his heart healed was what she longed for. He was her man, her husband, her lover, ... and she believed there was nothing she could do.

Dear Jesus, John prayed, *there has to be something I ... no ... something You ... can do.*

John looked up and the bare wall caught his eye just as the iris appeared. Dilating, it allowed entry to Celestria and three-year-old Terisa, the Avery's first child, to step onto the bridge.

Terisa, wearing in a white frilly dress, was adorable. Her dark brown hair formed ringlets as it flowed about her shoulders.

At seeing Pastor Bauer, the little girl pulled free of Celestria's hand to run and jump into his arms.

"Uncle John!" Terisa kissed his cheek, "You know what? Celestria is teaching me times tables."

"At age three? My, you are a smart little girl, aren't you?"

Terisa gave him a severe look. "Uncle John, *I* am a *big* girl now." She twisted to point at her mother's round belly. "*That* guy is little."

John chuckled. "I stand corrected. You are, indeed, big, aren't you? I'll not soon make that mistake again."

"Promise?"

John nodded, kissed her cheek, and then set her down before turning to *Celestria's* avatar. "I see, Celestria, that you're dressing in a more *contemporary* fashion and less like an angel these days."

With an accepting smile, she politely dipped her head once. "That was Captain Ramona's idea, sir."

Ramona shrugged. "What can I say? I never got used to an angel on board, Celestria, but you've been a real friend."

"I can only imagine," John said.

Standing on a chair, little Teri peered out a window. The Dalvus Nebula, as close as it was, filled the entire view on that side of the ship. Sitting at the heart of Coalition Territory, it cradled Parandi, the capital planet; Atheron;

Chagwa; and a number of less important planets; and acting as a great barrier to the Providence Union.

Atheron's sun, though now at a great distance, was still the brightest star in the sky. What if they went back to Atheron? What if they sought out the Christians in Seychelles as Neil believed was necessary? What then?

John drew a breath and, in exasperation, released it slowly. There was no point to Neil's going back. What would it prove anyway?

"Look what God made, Uncle John," Teri said. "Isn't it pretty?"

Unencumbered by life's worries, she saw things as simple and uncomplicated. If only her dad could.

Just then, the wall irised open again and Neil stepped in. Kissing his wife, he gave her a hug. In the next instant Neil was at his daughter's side to share the moment. "Whatcha lookin' at, honey?"

Terisa started to hum, and then quietly broke into a little song. "Jesus loves me this I know ... for *that* tells me so."

John saw that Teri was pointing at the huge Dalvus Nebula ... but whatever she saw eluded him. He glanced at Neil, only to find anger filling his face. Neil shot an annoyed look at John, turned abruptly, and left the bridge again.

Ramona followed him, but only with her eyes.

It was tough, but John turned back to the nebula rather than chase the man down. And then he saw it as well. "Oh, man, how could I have missed that?" He drew an arm over Teri's shoulder and wondered how Neil had interpreted this; such a powerful image.

"*Cel*, all stop, please," Ramona said. She had seen the vision in the nebula when she stepped next to John.

A myriad of colors, shadows, and light, painted a picture of a hand reaching out toward them. Chagwa, blocking its own sun, was in shadow and, looking like a dark hole, seemed to pierce the hand's palm.

John realized that Neil's answer wasn't complex at all. All Neil needed was Jesus' love. His sacrifice enveloped everything it touched with pure righteousness.

The hand, palm up and pierced, could be seen only here, at this specific angle.

John recognized the star sitting atop the print of the extended forefinger. He knew Neil did as well.

It was Atheron.

But he couldn't figure why this image would upset Neil.

John understood Neil had never received the absolution he so desperately longed for, nor accepted the Lord's love he so greatly needed. It was well within Neil's reach; all he had to do was accept the forgiveness as meant for him.

Sighing, John refocused on the rest of his flock. "I have to show this to our passengers," he said turning on his heel. "Cargo bay."

The smooth, bare wall irised open and John

stepped through the circular portal. As it closed behind him, he went to the cargo bay's side door to open it so everyone could see out toward Dalvus.

The awestruck refugees gave a sudden, corporate gasp followed by total silence.

The picture painted in the nebula, although an illusion, seemed to say, "The price was paid, come."

But why would this view upset Neil? John dropped his eyes to ask God for the answer, and then looked up to see the hand afresh, but he received no response.

Chapter 26
Terisa

NEIL paced the ship several times, but found no release from his anger.

As he cut through the cargo bay, he heard the oohs and aahs of the passengers speaking in hushed reverent whispers of God's grace regarding the scene before them. All he saw was an accusatory pointing finger demanding justice.

An hour had passed since he was last on the bridge, but he had no desire to go there. Instead he took his anger with him all the way to his daughter's room, but he buried it before peeking in.

She was back from the bridge, and he found her focused on a figurine of some sort. Her long, curly, dark hair contrasting with the white chiffon dress her mother had just finished, made her look like a porcelain doll as she sat at the base of her chest of drawers.

"Whatcha got there?"

Terisa looked up and stared at him with eyes that said, oh, oh, I've been caught. "I just wanted to look at this, Daddy. Now it's broke."

Neil stepped into the room. Terisa held up the statuette that had once topped his wedding cake. Ramona treasured the china piece for a reason. Carl Ogier had removed the original ornaments—*separate figures of a bride and groom*—and had replaced them with this *one*; a single ornament of a groom embracing his bride. Connected only from the waist up, the kiss, sweet and innocent, implied a perfect union.

He took a seat on her bed as she got to her feet and handed two pieces to him. The groom had been snapped in half at the waist.

"Honey, you weren't supposed to take this without asking. It's not a toy. It belongs to Mom. You have to give it back."

"I know, Daddy. I'm sorry I broke it. I can't give it back to Mommy like this."

"What do you want me to do with it?"

"Daddy, I want you to fix it please."

Neil pressed the groom's lower half to the upper to study the damage. Although it was a clean break, Neil never had any luck with this sort of thing.

He remembered one of his mother's figurines suffering a similar fate after an illicit *in-the-house*, ill-thrown baseball got away from him. With glue everywhere, and the damage growing worse with his every attempt to fix it, the ornament ended up looking like a poorly constructed three-D jigsaw puzzle. Hiding it and himself in his room in the hopes Mom's favorite Hummel wouldn't be missed was probably not the best choice a ten-year-old could have made. The resulting spanking wouldn't have been as severe had he fessed up to begin with, as his buddy Dennis Dugan had suggested.

"I don't think I can fix this, sweet cheeks. Glue and I always seem at odds with each other.

You just need to take this back to Mommy and explain." He tried to hand the pieces back to her but, met with such grief-stricken eyes, he felt his heart skip a beat.

"Daddy, you can fix it. You have too."

His little girl had Mom's eyes. Dark brown and compelling, they had a way of obligating him to impossible tasks in spite of himself.

"Okay, honey, but give me time. I want to do it right, okay?"

Her gaze held just a hint of suspicion as she brought her face just inches from his. "*You* fix it, Daddy. Not *Celestria*, okay?"

"I was thinking *Cel* might do a better job."

"No, Daddy. Your hands only please. Your hands have more love in them."

Neil chuckled. "They do?"

Unexpectedly, Terisa' eyes filled with tears and she lurched into his embrace. "You're my daddy. You've got more love in your hands than anybody. You have to fix it, you just have to."

Neil held her close as his mind raced in search of a way out of this, but he found none. "Okay, baby girl. I'll do my best."

"Promise?" Holding him tight, she was reluctant to let go.

Finally focused on what was actually taking place, Neil pushed everything else from his mind and just held her, giving her all the time and attention she needed.

After a long moment, she kissed his cheek and pulled away.

His cheeks pulled into an honest smile all on their own. He kissed her forehead, crossed his heart, and said, "I promise, okay? I'll do it for you."

As she nodded, Neil saw that the trust in her large, dark, eyes would hold him to his pledge. "Thank you, Daddy."

"Terisa, I'm going to require payment though."

Her eyes lit up. "Okay." She quickly pulled open the top drawer of her dresser, brought out a sock and from it dumped three coins into her hand. "I got lots of money. You can have it all, Daddy." She then plopped three Providence pennies into his palm.

Wide eyed, brows arched high; Neil looked at the coins and shook his head. "I'm sorry, but this is not nearly enough, honey. This won't do at all."

She cocked her head. "I saved this from Christmas. It's all I have. I don't have any more money, Daddy."

Neil gently took her hand, set the coins in it, and curled her fingers around them. "My price is *two* great big hugs. One now and one when I've finished. I know the amount is steep but—"

Terisa threw her arms around his neck nearly strangling him in her embrace. "I love you, Daddy." He was her hero, or was supposed to be anyway, and now he was committed to facing his old enemy, glue.

He kissed her cheek and took the pieces to

the small repair shop just off the cargo bay. Pushing his helmet aside, he set the figurine pieces on the counter. His helmet now had more than half the hashes painted over with white.

"I wish Carl were here. Lucky stiff, gallivanting around the 'verse ... saving folks. Oh, well. The kid makes a great Paladin; I just wonder how well he and glue get along."

"I hear he's working on Atheron as we speak."

Neil turned to find Celestria standing in the doorway. "I'm not going back there to hunt him down just to fix this." He thought about it for a moment before shrugging off the notion.

"Cel, do we have a proper adhesive for this?"

"One moment, sir."

In another instant, a small door opened on a cabinet's face. From inside Neil pulled out a small tube of glue. "Thanks, Cel."

A vision popped into his head niggling at his already heightened apprehension; a picture of himself, hands dripping with adhesive, and stuck fast to a cabinet door.

From a retractable arm, a magnifying glass hung below an upper cabinet. Neil used it to see the glue tube's label. "Oh, great. Even that mocks me."

Celestria's label read, "Adhesive for Neil."

With a tightened jaw, he faced this enemy with great deference.

"Let's see ... Just unscrew the lid, and dab a

drop here and here." Neil replaced the lid and brought the figurine's lower half carefully to the upper. "Perfect."

If not for a faint but visible seam, the joint was faultless. Nothing he couldn't live with at any rate, but what would Ramona think?

Careful to check for stray glue on his fingertips, Neil slid the little cake topper to the countertop's back edge.

From this distance the bride and groom looked perfect. No one would notice the groom's flaw, no one but Neil that is. Neil pulled a bar stool close, sat on it, and leaned on the counter to admire his work, but something about the figurine made his brow stiffen. If it weren't for the sentimental value he and Ramona held for it, he would have tossed it against the wall.

He turned away, but the tightness in his forehead spread to his temples. Neil threw up his hands in resignation.

Actually, what the figurine represented was most fitting; a flawed groom ... a flawless bride ... forever joined.

He slammed a fist against the wall but was too furious to feel any pain.

A nonchalant "Ouch," came from the doorway. Celestria, now leaning on the doorjamb, had her arms folded.

"I'm sorry, Cel."

"It's okay, sir. I'm sure your anger wasn't aimed at me." She slid a box of tissues his way.

Neil gave the box a puzzled look. "What's that for?" And then he noticed his cheeks were wet. Had he been crying? He must have been so riled up he hadn't noticed that either.

"Can you tell me what's got you upset, sir."

He shrugged. "I don't know. I guess it's that stupid thing." He shot a thumb over his shoulder toward the porcelain piece. It represents Ramona and me pretty well, don't you think?"

She pushed herself from the door jam, stepped forward, and took the piece in hand to study it more closely.

"This is a cake decoration." Her tone said she attributed no more to it than that.

Neil rolled his head to loosen stiff neck muscles before letting out a long sigh.

As the avatar admired the figurine, a smile began to lift her cheeks. "Terisa will be so happy that you fixed it."

Neil stood abruptly, snatched the small statue from her grasp, and threw it with all his might at the far wall.

Celestria, instantly there before it connected with the bulkhead, caught it with one hand.

With a clamped jaw, Neil glared at her in exasperation. There was no beating someone who could disappear and reappear somewhere else in a heartbeat. And less of a chance with someone who could appear in two places at once. The blasted holographic avatar was there before it left his hand. He turned to leave, but *that* Celestria blocked his way.

"It's a cake decoration, sir. Why are you portraying it as something beyond that?"

He glanced away and shook his head. Why was he letting it affect him more than it should? It was just a keepsake, a little porcelain memory of a significant day, nothing more. He took a deep breath and released it hard.

The second avatar, from behind him, held the statuette over his shoulder. "Here you go, sir. Terisa will be so happy to have it back."

Neil yanked it from her grasp, half glanced at it and then looked again. The groom was flawed—so what? Realistically the tiny crease was hardly noticeable across the once smooth, jet-black porcelain tuxedo.

"Cel, I'm sure Terisa expected more from me. My hands only, she said. But that's the best it'll be. I'm no miracle worker."

"No, sir. You're not. You are an imperfect human who has needs just like everyone else. No one expects you to be perfect—no one."

He checked it once more under the magnifier, but the crack remained. Oh, well … It wasn't going to get any better. Ramona would notice, but maybe she would accept it anyway. She had accepted *him* with all his flaws, why wouldn't she accept this?

"May I ask you something, Captain?"

"Sure, Cel." He looked up at the Avatar's expressionless face.

"Do you think Ramona is without her faults … even with God's hand on her?" And with that, both avatars merged into one, then vanished.

Neil ran his thumb over the porcelain. The seam felt deeper than it looked.

Just then, Terisa burst in, panting hard. "Daddy! … Mommy's … having … the baby."

Neil stuffed the porcelain figurine into a pocket, snatched up the three-year-old, called for the infirmary, then stepped through the iris into the hallway just outside it.

He let Teri down in the hall. "Cel?"

The avatar appeared before then. "Sir?"

"Take care of Teri, please."

"Certainly, sir."

Neil knelt before Teri, pulled the cake topper from his pocket, and handed it to her. "Teri, take this and go with Celestria."

Wide-eyed, she looked at the porcelain piece for only a brief moment before throwing her arms around his neck. "Thank you, Daddy."

Neil kissed her cheek, stood, then stepped into the room.

Margery Barrett, a practiced midwife, had Ramona sitting erect on a birthing bed. Its back was mostly upright, as near chair-like as Margery could get it.

Ramona, already red-faced with labor pains, motioned to Neil to come closer so she could take his hand.

THIRTEEN hours later, Neil stepped from the room, and braced himself on a wall.

The labor started poorly and had gotten worse with each passing minute despite Mrs. Barrett and the avatar's best efforts.

Approaching total exhaustion, and barely audible, Ramona called for her mother.

Celestria agreed with Mrs. Barrett's assessment, this might be the last chance Ramona and her parents would have to see each other. Making that happen fell squarely on Neil's shoulders.

"*Celestria*, turn us around and get us back to Atheron as fast as you can."

The avatar appeared before him. "Where would you like me to set down?"

"Get us back to Seychelles and hide in the woods just north of the village. Hurry."

"Yes, sir. Teri's awake. I'll take her with me to the bridge."

"Please. Just don't alarm her."

"I'll let her pretend she's the pilot."

Neil nodded and watched the avatar head away. *Celestria* had played 'little girl pilot' with his daughter before. Good, Teri would be occupied with matters other than her mother's condition. He turned his attention back to his wife.

Chapter 27

Mr. and Mrs. French

SHORT, green grass, a few low lying shrubs, rays of sunbeams filtering through the aspen trees would have made for a tranquil scene if it weren't for the knot in the pit of Neil's stomach.

He checked his personal holo-emitter, a three-inch disk clipped to his belt that hid his identity under his latest disguise, that of an elderly nondescript man. As far as anyone could tell, he could have been anything from a schoolteacher to a used skitter salesman. He chose this face mainly because it appeared kind and harmless whether he smiled or scowled.

He stepped next to the last aspen at the edge of the woods. Behind him, *Celestria* was well hidden in a tight grove. The forest he was in and Seychelles village in the valley below were separated by an easy rolling hill. One lone sentinel, a tall, broad oak stood at the hill's crest to mark the dirt trail for his return.

Beyond Seychelles, in the middle of a farmer's field, the mammoth, raggedy-edge remains of the *Emperor's Princess* jutted fifteen stories into the sky. For more than a moment, Neil recalled his following the burning hulk in his Dart all the way to the planet' surface.

As he followed the dirt path that meandered down the slope to the village, he noted that it was well traveled. Still, it didn't lead straight to the ship, and *Cel* knew how to protect herself, anyway.

A myriad of things could go wrong. Atheron continued to be on high alert with increased patrols combing every street. Ramona's shooting an officer in their escape didn't help matters either.

But still, he believed his disguise was perfect. Who'd suspect an old man enjoying a morning stroll through the streets of Seychelles? He entered the village. Ramona's folks, now five years past her abduction by a rogue Enforcer, should no longer be on the Coalition's 'Suspects' list, or so he hoped.

The streets were clean for the most part, belying the suffocating oppression Neil knew everyone lived under. He found the French's family home on a pristine side street amid similar picket fenced houses.

Down the road another three blocks, sat the tavern where Ramona had worked, and Neil could now feel his heart pulse in his throat as memories of his first visit pressed to the forefront of his thoughts.

He considered her folks' home, a small Government Issue Cape Cod. Folks were allowed to fix them up somewhat, but …

Ramona's folks had pushed right up to approved limits with fresh paint and plant life.

Standing at the head of the walkway to the front door of the French's house, Neil went over the speech he had prepared, but it now seemed rather stupid.

He ducked under the vine-covered trellised archway and cautiously headed up the walk to their front door. Heart pounding, he wanted to rush in shouting, ... but to call out *what* exactly?

"Hello," he heard a voice call, and looked up to see a dark-haired woman in her late forties standing in the house's open door. She looked very much like Ramona. "Can I help you, sir?" she asked with a kind smile.

Neil felt himself freeze as a torrent of conflicting emotions flooded his mind. He glanced back up the street toward the hill and its distant lone oak. So much stood in the way of the mission he had set for himself. Did the French's still love their daughter? They had to, he assured himself. How could they not? Would their love for Ramona be strong enough to bridge the five-year gap without an explanation? Would they trust him enough to come? Their daughter was now in far more danger than she had ever been. They simply must come.

"Sir, are you all right?" She took a step down her stoop and beckoned with a quick jerk of her head just as Ramona would have done, "Got a hot pot brewed and some apple crumb cake aching to be sliced."

He stepped closer but didn't take her outstretched hand. "I would like that. Thank you."

She led him into the kitchen where an aroma of coffee and fresh baked cake greeted him. An older man wearing wire framed glasses, sitting at the table put down his *Seychelles' Sentinel* news pad. "And you are, sir?"

The woman turned away to pull a cup and small plate from a cupboard.

Neil hesitated, and then nervously blurted, "Are you Mr. and Mrs. French?" With that, and the startled look of the couple, his mind went blank.

With knit brow, Mr. French leaned toward the stranger in his home. "Who are you?"

Just then, *Celestria's* voice whispered in Neil's earpiece, "Say nothing, sir. You're being monitored. There's a truck down the block loaded with high-tech equipment. But I believe it's audio only."

"Ave... Aven... Avenshire. Tom Avenshire, sir," Neil stuttered, as he took a seat.

"What do you want, Mr. Avenshire?"

"I bring word of ..." Neil thought quickly "... the parcel of land you were interested in. It's now on the market,"

Neil put a finger to his lips, and then knocked the sugar bowl spilling some of its contents on the table. Apologizing for his clumsiness, he wrote "Ramona" in the spilled sugar, and then wiped the writing away.

"She lives?" Mr. French mouthed silently.

Neil nodded, and glanced at Mrs. French who now covered her mouth with a trembling hand. The message in the sugar must have been bittersweet for her.

"Well, uh, Jean and I are interested in that parcel, if it's the one we think it is. When can we see it again?"

"I've got a little time right now," Neil said. "What say we take a look?"

"Men approach," whispered *Celestria*. "Go out the back way *now*."

Neil sprang to his feet, and gestured that someone was coming in the front entrance. Heading for the back door, he motioned that the older couple should follow him. The Frenchs quickly obeyed his non-verbal instructions.

Celestria's voice guided him through back alleyways, side streets, and even a storm drain culvert, past patrols, to the edge of town.

Now for the most dangerous leg back to the ship. Neil gazed up at the lone oak, the dirt trail to it, and noted the meadow. No cover at all, he thought. Now what?

"*Celestria*, we can't get to you without being seen. Any advice?"

"I have an idea, Daddy." Teri's voice was confident. "One moment please."

As they hunkered down behind some thick bushes, a troop transport came around the corner and passed right by them.

"*Cel*, we're cut off. The terrain's too open between us and you."

"There's less traffic south of you, Daddy. If you can make it to the *Princess*, we can pick you up there."

"Roger, Teri. On our way."

217

Neil, with *Celestria's* help, guided the older couple through the less used streets and back alleys until they reached the tavern.

Mr. French caught hold of Neil's arm to get his attention. "This is where it all began, sir. This is where our daughter was …"

Studying the old man's eyes for a brief moment, Neil patted his shoulder reassuringly. "Yes, I know," he said, then took them around the back toward the downed cruise liner, before stopping at the alley's end.

This was the very path he followed to lead Ramona to safety and, indeed, five years hadn't changed the landscape much, that is, until he came around the last building. The last time around, the *Emperor's Princess* lay smoldering under smoke so thick it choked out the sun.

But on this bright and beautiful day, vine, tree, and bush cloaked the ruins in soft shades of green. Even at this distance, another three hundred yards or so, small flowers of yellow, white, and pink, polka dotting the bushes, painted a surreal scene. It seemed as though God, with nature, was reclaiming His own.

Celestria's tone was urgent. "Men ahead, sir."

Neil turned back.

"The alley's blocked from behind as well," she added.

"*Cel*, you're not making this easy," Neil scolded.

"Sorry, sir. Something's interfering with my

218

scanners. I didn't see them."

Neil motioned the Frenchs to take cover, and as they hurried to crouch behind a dumpster, he checked his gun, tucked it back into and under the holo-camouflage and braced himself for a shootout.

Just then, two Enforcers rounded the corner cutting off his path to safety. Behind him, two more blocked his escape.

"You there!" said one. "There's a curfew. What are you doing out here?"

"Sorry, sir. Just taking out the trash." Neil stepped away from the dumpster, dusted off his hands, and motioned to a building's back door.

The Enforcer, hand on his holster, nodded.

Neil walked to the door he'd indicated and took the knob and jostled it. It was locked.

"Blasted thing gets stuck sometimes." He smiled nervously at the Enforcers, and jostled the knob again. "Come on, not now."

"Show your papers. Identify yourself."

Neil hesitated. *Celestria* had long ago removed the ident-chip that had been imbedded in the back of his hand. He hoped the one now glued to his palm in his clenched fist would fool the scanner.

Palm down, he held out his hand. The Enforcer stepped forward, scanned it, then checked the reading. "You're clear. Now get inside before I arrest you."

Neil tugged at the door again and then forcefully rattled it, but it didn't open. "Must've locked myself out. Sorry, gents."

Just then the door swung inward and a lady stood in the threshold blocking his path.

"Locked myself out again, honey," he said as he tried to step past her, but she barred his way.

"I don't know you, Mister," she said firmly with a hand on his chest.

"Ah, come on, honey bunches. I said I was sorry. Please, let me in before these fine gentlemen think ill of me. You don't want me to spend another night in jail, do you?"

Looking past him to the Enforcer, she refused to let him in. "Officers, I don't know this man."

Glancing at the Enforcers, Neil released a nervous chuckle. "Hildagard has got a powerful grudge brewin', boys. Oh, well, seems my bed and a square is at your house tonight."

"Hildegard?" she bellowed. "Name's Letti … Letti Graves. You can check that yourself, officer." She held out her hand to be scanned.

Suddenly, Neil bolted past her, pushing her out of harm's way into the apartment, spun and fired at the Enforcers. Two dropped where they stood, stunned by Neil's zithion-charged rubber bullets.

The other two Enforcers fired as Neil ducked for cover behind a couch, but an errant bullet caught him in the hip. He reeled and writhed at the sudden jolt, but found enough presence to attack.

He popped up and fired twice, but the Enforcers, still outside, had little reason to show themselves. Help … *their help*, would soon be on its way.

Just then, both men collapsed, crumpling to the ground. Someone peeked in but, backlit by the bright noonday sun, Neil couldn't make out who it might be.

"Hello," the newcomer called into the house. "You okay?"

"Who's there?"

"Tennyson, Tony Tennyson."

Neil got to his feet and headed for the door, brushing past the woman who now stood motionless, clearly paralyzed by all the gunplay. "For your own sake, lady, you best forget this day completely."

With brows arched high, she gave her head a rapid nervous jerk, and then locked the door behind him as Neil stepped out into the daylight.

Carlton Ogier, wearing a full beard, checked both ends of the alley with a gun at the ready then glanced at Neil. "That's not much of a disguise, Captain Star."

Neil looked down; his holographic disguise was gone. He was unharmed by the Enforcer's bullet, but the holo-emitter sputtered random sparks before dying completely, having given its life to save his.

"Yeah, well, I hadn't time to grow a beard, Mr. Tennyson." Neil said. "Glad you made it."

"I've got your wing, Cap. I always have."

Carl's just in the nick of time arrival surprised Neil, but he had no time to think about it. He patted Carl's shoulder, brushed past him, and then went to the dumpster to bring out Mr. and Mrs. French. "Let's go."

Mr. French jerked back. Wide eyed, he fumed, "I recognize *you*, you murdering piece of filth. I'm not going anywhere with you."

Neil turned and scowled at the man. "We don't have time for this. For Ramona's sake, as well as your own, you have to come with me." Neil grabbed his arm.

The old man recoiled and wrenched from Neil's grasp.

Carl stepped forward. "You've got to trust us, Mr. French. There's no other choice."

"Back off! I'm not goi—"

Neil caught the older man's jaw with a clenched fist. He crumpled. Neil hoisted him over his shoulder as Carl took hold of Mrs. French's arm. Together, they hurried across the street and headed for the *Princess*.

Without warning, shots rang out and bullets ricocheted off the road near their feet. Neil turned to see an armored troop transport barrel down the street toward them and then abruptly skid to a stop. They fired again, but their bullets now bounced off something invisible; a barrier between them and Neil.

Under cover of *Level-A Stealth*, *Celestria* had come to bar the truck's advance opposite her, and then lowered a welcoming ramp.

Chapter 28

The Awakening

A SHARP whine in Tobin French's ears tugged him from unconsciousness. He jerked awake, nearly toppling from his bed, but steadying hands caught him.

"Easy, Mr. French." The masculine voice sounded familiar.

He opened his eyes and tried to focus. Someone handed him his glasses. He put them on, blinked, and saw the blond, bearded man from the alley.

"You!"

"Name's Carl, sir. I mean you no harm."

Tobin raised his head to see he was in a medical room of some sort. A computer-generated display on one wall flashed with indicator lights, showing labels, readings, and graphs, all moving in rhythm. "What's all that?"

"Your vitals."

He could see his pulse and read his blood pressure in real time. This was like nothing he'd ever seen before. It was beyond modern, beyond anything the Coalition could contrive.

He sat up and dropped his legs from the bed, and with that his head nearly exploded.

"Take it slow, sir. Neil hit you pretty hard."

"Neil?" He looked up at Carl's concern filled face. "Neil Avery?"

Carl focused on him. "You know Neil?"

Tobin rubbed his forehead. "Got anything for pain?"

"*Celestria*, can you help this man?"

"Yes, sir."

Tobin heard a high-pitched tone, then his ears popped and his head cleared.

"Ouch, what was that?"

"Mr. French," Carl said, ignoring Tobin's question, "how do you know Neil Avery?"

Tobin spoke without looking up. "After Mona's disappearance—*after her abduction*—the man's picture was all over the news. Killed by pirates while on maneuvers, they said. He was a fallen hero, they said. Yeah, some hero. He was credited with putting down a Christian infiltration on the *Emperor's Princess*; Trog terrorists trying to make landfall, so said those lying ..."

Tobin peered at Carl over his wire-rimmed glasses. "Five years ... for five years I believed my daughter was dead ... or worse. Stolen away by that scum and later taken by pirates maybe. Now to find she lives? Where is she? Where's my daughter?"

"Her condition is serious, sir. She's giving birth, or trying to. There is a very real chance that she won't make it. The labor has been difficult. That's why we brought you here."

"Who's with her?"

"She has a skilled midwife attending her. Your wife is there. Just seeing her mother has helped—to see you will even more so."

Tobin jumped to his feet and nearly toppled with a sudden dizzy spell. Carl steadied him.

Like a tornado pushing everything else aside, Tobin's mind forced a single thought to the forefront—to demand an answer. Was his daughter Avery's slave or—*God forbid*—his wife? Tobin couldn't bring himself to ask. In either case, the news was sure to twist the knot in his stomach tighter than it already was.

"Did you say she might not make it? If she's having that butcher's child, maybe her death would be a good thing."

"What? How could you possibly say that? She's your daughter."

"Do *you* have any children, Carl?

"No, I haven't been so blessed."

"Then you couldn't possibly understand a father's concern. I know my daughter would want nothing to do with an Enforcer, especially *that* murderer."

"There is so much you don't get. It's not like that. Mona loves him."

"If that's true then I can't understand any of this. Why didn't she contact us during these last five years? What happened to the ideals her mother and I taught her? How could she love someone like that? Did he do something to her mind? None of this is right."

"Nothing like that happened. Mr. French, I can truthfully tell you Mona missed you deeply."

"And I her, Carl." All of this seemed like a

horrible nightmare.

Just then a little girl came into the room, saw he was up, and ran to hug him. "Granpa, you're awake."

Granpa? Tobin thought as he glanced at Carl, then back to the child as his gut twisted a notch. The very idea that *his* little girl had willingly married a mass murderer sickened him. He took a deep breath and released it slowly, all the while automatically embracing the child in his arms.

Tobin pulled back from the little girl and set her on her feet to get a better look at the youngster. "And who might you be?"

The girl beamed and spoke with pride. "I'm your granddaughter, Terisa Breanna Avery."

He surged to his feet. "And the child she bares now, also his?" he asked of no one in particular.

He stepped past Terisa and Carl without another word and headed down the hallway only to find himself standing at the entrance to a huge room. It was full of cots and luggage, and dozens, no, hundreds of people in small groups on their knees.

"Who are all these people? More victims?"

"Refugees, Mr. French," Carl said from behind him. "It's what the Averys' do; rescue people. It's what your son-in-law lives for."

Tobin turned to face the bearded blond. "He torpedoed the *Princess* into oblivion, killing thousands of innocents—my own sister among them, … her husband, … my nephew." Tobin glowered at Carl. "And now, out of the blue, you ask me to accept my daughter's kidnapper as my son? Well, isn't that something? You might as well rip my heart from my chest. There's no way in this lifetime or in the next will I accept that monster as my son."

Carl stepped forward and for a long moment said nothing. When he finally spoke, his tone was a calm, sober whisper. "She chose him for reasons you don't yet understand. I know. I was there. You have to forgive him, Mr. French. He *is* Ramona's husband."

"I *have* to do nothing of the sort! For five years she was dead to me. Maybe it should've stayed that way." Tobin glared at Carl meaning every word.

Carl straightened his shoulders and squared his jaw. "You have no right to …"

Turning away, tears blurred Tobin's eyes. "I prayed I'd see her again, hoping beyond hope that somehow my daughter had survived. And now, I can't stand the thought of being with her knowing she married that … that …"

"Oh, this is real peachy," Carl said. "I suppose you can't pick your relatives, can you? Sometimes you wind up with real slime bags."

Tobin turned to Carl. The youngish, blond's eyes were now filled with disgust. With arms folded, Carl stood straight and defiant.

Tobin turned to face Carl straight on. "I may have issues with my daughter, but I'll not have you speaking of her like that."

"Oh, I wasn't taking about her; it's you I have concerns with. I'm forever surprised with just how mean a man can be. But you? You have got to be the world champ."

"Who are you to judge? The man she married is a—"

"Kind and generous soul. Yeah, I know him, but obviously you don't."

"I was about to say—"

"Your ignorance was about to spout trash. Ask me and I'll tell you about Neil … the Neil you don't know. But before you speak, know this, if you ever butcher your daughter's reputation in front of me again, I'll hurt you … and you can take that to the bank. She lies in the infirmary, in trouble, needing you, and you can't get beyond your own prejudices."

With that, Carl turned and headed away.

"No! Wait!" Tobin hurried to his side, but Carl kept walking. "Tell me then; who is Neil Avery? How do you know him?"

Ignoring his question, Carl went to a closed door. "Mr. French, there's no telling how well she's fairing. Do you really want your feelings for Neil to bar you from your daughter now?"

"Answer my questions!" Tobin snapped.

Carl glared at him. "Questions? There's no time for questions. Go to your daughter!"

Tobin glanced away and released a sigh. "I can't believe my daughter married … *him*."

Carl rested a reassuring hand on Tobin's

shoulder. "The questions can wait. Mona needs her father now. You may never get another chance to do right by her, so don't blow this … this answer to your prayers."

Tobin dropped his gaze.

"When you're ready," Carl said, "pass a hand over that sensor. The door will slide open." Carl turned away and headed down the hall.

Tobin fell against the door jam, tears falling like rain. He didn't know her story, not yet anyway, but maybe it was … He steeled himself to be strong; to be strong for Ramona's sake. Maybe her story was … God's.

Wiping his eyes with a sleeve, he squared his shoulders, and waved a hand across the sensor.

Tilted forward in a near sitting position, Ramona, pale and sweating profusely, strained in labor. Next to her, Neil Avery clutched her hand, a mix of concern and encouragement on his face. Two women, one standing between Ramona's feet, the other standing behind the first, encouraged Ramona to push. Jean, Mona's mother, stood next to Ramona, opposite Neil.

With an abrupt hiss, the door closed behind Tobin. He stepped in and took a place by his wife's side to take his daughter's free hand. "Ramona? I'm here, honey."

Now sixteen hours into labor, Mona was running out of energy. She met his eyes with a tiny smile of delight, but her tired expression told the real story.

Tobin leaned close. "You can do this, honey. God is with you."

"I see the top of his head, Mona," the midwife said. "Push, girl, push."

"I'll try, Margery." Ramona strained, her face flushing red as she bore down, and then she fell back, too weak to do more.

"Don't give up, my wife," Neil insisted. "Reach down and find the strength you need. Push!"

Mona gritted her teeth and bore down.

The baby's head appeared.

Mona collapsed.

Neil embraced her, desperate to lend his strength to hers. "I love you, honey."

Neil truly loved Mona. Tobin could see that, but there was more to their relationship. Neil shared a connection to his wife that few men enjoy with their own. Most don't even know such things can exist. At Neil's touch strength seemed to flow into Mona.

Tobin marveled at what he saw; words failing to describe what he now knew to be true. His mind awakened to a reality he had never before encountered—the presence of an intense Someone who, like mortar joining bricks, cemented this young couple together.

As Mona looked up into her husband's eyes, renewed power and purpose brought color to her cheeks.

She pushed again.

Chapter 29

A Plunge into Icy Water

TOBIN stepped from the room.

Carl lay stretched out on a cushioned bench in the hallway, but sat up when Tobin came out. "How is she, Mr. French?"

Tobin glanced back at the closed door. "It was a hard labor—healthy baby boy—but she may not ..." The words caught in his throat. No, he'd not give voice to doubt, not now. "Mona just needs to rest, that's all. She'll be fine."

Carl forced a smile. "Sure she will. I'm convinced of it."

"About Neil ... You say you know him?"

"For five years now." Carl got to his feet and gestured toward the far end of the hall to a side room, a repair shop off the cargo bay. He picked up a helmet that sat on a corner of the counter-top and handed it to Tobin.

"What's this?" the older man asked, not understanding Carl's action. Someone had done a poor job painting over more than half the black marks with white paint. "You must have known Avery before the *Princess* was destroyed."

"I did. That helmet, those hashes are the reason Neil was the way he was." Carl looked away and rubbed his face with a firm hand before looking back at Tobin. "Yeah, I knew him. He was my squadron leader."

"No wonder you're defending him. You're as bad as—"

"There were times when I couldn't stand looking into the man's eyes either. But that's only because in them I saw my future; I saw my eyes in five years time, devoid of life. I suppose that's what I hated the most; the thought of winding up like that. But I was with him on that mission. I flew his wing, Mr. French."

Tobin couldn't hide his disappointment in Carl. "Oh, I see," he said, at once discounting anything else the man might say.

"No, sir, you don't see. In each *Dart* fighter there is a small screen dedicated to your partner's face. As I watched Neil, I saw a change take place that surprised me. To handle the tight turns and such, a pilot has to have a concentrated focus and strong stomach, but as we dove on the *Princess*, before we launched that first torpedo or fired the first shot, I saw Neil turn pale. He looked as though he was about to pass out."

"So?"

"Look at those hashes. At one time there were better than five hundred, each representing a kill. Though he was a seasoned soldier, it was all he could do to follow his orders this time."

"He could have disobeyed them. He had a choice."

"He could have …" Carl's gaze was intense as he considered Tobin "… but he would have died in the attempt, and the attack would have continued anyway."

"How do you mean?"

"It's the way strikes are set up. His *Dart* was in Lt. Troy Younger's crosshairs."

"Excuse me?"

"Troy was Neil's second in command. Had Neil veered away or failed to launch that first torpedo, Troy was duty bound to kill him. And Troy would have done it without thinking twice. For Troy, it would have meant his immediate promotion to captain."

"Bad guy was he ... this Troy fella. *Even* for an Enforcer?"

Carl half nodded. "To say the least. Unlike Neil, or myself, Troy loved to kill, and he didn't give one wit about innocence or guilt. He and Neil were like brothers once, but despite that, Troy would have ended Neil in a heartbeat."

"So I'm to forgive Neil Avery despite that downing?"

"You're a stubborn man, Mr. French. Look at that helmet. Neil has tried to backtrack his killing the only way he knows how. Each painted over hash mark represents a life saved since the downing.

He still thinks in terms of an eye-for-an-eye, and hasn't gotten hold of Christ's saving Grace. You're just like him in that regard."

Tobin looked away. "A price has to be paid for what he did. Someone has to pay for that ship's destruction."

"Someone already has. The real culprit is

behind bars. As far as Neil is concerned, let me remind you of St. Paul on the road to Damascus. He too was a murderer of Christians; thought he was doing God's work, until he met Christ on that dirt road. It took Paul better than eighteen years to get the Christians in Jerusalem to see he had changed. Eighteen years is a long time, Mr. French. Don't make the man wait. You, sir, aren't that important in the vast scheme of things."

That pricked, but Tobin couldn't refute Carl's reasoning. Who was he to deny Neil what Christ had so freely given.

Tobin still needed to build a bridge back to his daughter. Maybe confronting Neil, no, maybe *talking* to him ... He owed his daughter at least that much anyway.

"Where's Neil now?"

"*Celestria?*"

"Captain Avery is in the hall, sir, showing the baby to Terisa."

Tobin turned away, took a couple reluctant steps before glancing back at Carl. "Trying to be a man of God, is he?"

Carl gestured toward the door. "See for yourself."

Tobin looked at the helmet once more before tossing it to Carl.

Drawing a deep breath as if he were about to take a plunge into icy water, he released it slowly, and then stepped into the hallway. The door hissed closed behind him.

Chapter 30

The Wingman

HOLDING his newborn, wrapped in a soft light blue blanket, Neil knelt before his daughter in the hallway. "Teri, this is your baby brother, Douglas Taylor Avery. What do you think of him?"

Terisa gently pulled the blanket away from Baby Douglas' red face to admire him. "Oh, Daddy. That's a fine baby boy. But he better know who's in charge; I was here first.

Neil chuckled.

"Daddy?"

"Yeah, hon?"

"What if something's wrong with him? Are you still going to keep him?"

Neil chuckled again. "Oh … flaws and all, no matter what, he's my son, and I'll always cherish him, just as I will always love you."

"No matter what?"

"No matter what."

No matter what? came another voice.

Startled, Neil turned. No one there. Though this was the first time he'd heard this voice, it came with a sense of recognition.

No matter what? he heard again, but it wasn't a voice—*not really*—and yet it was. It was more of a feeling … an unction … a direct connection to the speaker, bypassing every sense Neil understood.

Yes. I will love my son forever. Neil responded in thought alone.

You are my son, and I love you far more than you love little Douglas.

A torrent of guilt and horrible images sprang into Neil's mind. The inferno in the sky, charred remains of people, faces twisted in excruciating agony on the decks of the *Emperor's Princess*, flaming chunks of metal falling to the earth; filled Neil's thoughts. His involuntary gasp accompanied a stab of agony.

No, my son. As if swept away by a breath, the awful images vanished like smoke. Instantly, Neil saw into the *Princess* before the attack. Three-thousand-twenty-four souls walking her decks; some among them openly preaching the Word of God. Inexplicably, Neil knew each and every one of the individuals by name, and understood why each was on the ship. One in particular, a boy, preached as if on fire. Passengers were in tears, some on their knees, as the power of God covered the entire ship.

In the last few hours that remained before the attack, God had sent his people, including Proctor McCullough, into the decks to preach the good news and, before meeting their end, most of the men, women, and children accepted Christ as Lord and Savior.

Not everyone was saved, but every person was given the chance.

Neil knew also that each of those Christians had boarded knowing they might never make landfall, but they went anyway.

Dropping to his knees with his baby boy in his arms, Neil suddenly felt surrounded by pure encompassing acceptance bathing every dark nook of his soul. More than acceptance though; Neil struggled to define it, understand it, this thing far greater than … Ah, yes. Love. Pure. Simple in substance, complex in its effect. Without reservation Love touched him, wrapped him, flowed through him, carrying him to a place above and beyond his present perception.

Neil before God began to see the depth, the breadth, and the height of Jesus' love, and he laughed—laughed at his own inability to find its limits. But now he knew, now he could see that it was for this reason that God gave His only begotten Son, that no man should perish, but have everlasting life, even Neil Avery.

Laughing uncontrollably, Neil opened his tear-filled eyes to find he was sprawled on his back.

Standing above him, with the baby now safely held in his arms, a puzzled Mr. French scowled down at him. "What are you doing?"

But Neil didn't answer—couldn't answer. Still simultaneously laughing and crying, he carefully climbed to his feet, weak-kneed, and wobbled past Mr. French and Teri to the front lounge. Beyond the window, vivid and striking, he saw the hand of God as if for the first time. It wasn't the pointing finger of accusation Neil had seen previously, but an outstretched, inviting hand, pierced at the palm; and, falling to his knees, Neil began to cry even harder.

He looked back and, through blurred eyes, saw his baby boy safe in his father-in-law's arms and realized that, in God's hands, he, too, was safe. Neil felt restored.

He steadied himself, clutching the window frame, and saw his reflection in the glass, a stupid, drunken grin spread across his filthy, moist-from-tears face. Ruffled hair was the least of his problems. The suit he'd worn all day was covered with dirt and dust. Disheveled from the foray in the alley, its shoulder had a rip in the seam. His tie hung loose. He had traveled far. And he certainly looked like a drunk.

Mr. French, holding the baby, followed Teri into the lounge to where Neil stood.

"Daddy?" Teri turned his attention. "Are you okay?"

Neil knelt and drew one arm around his daughter. "Better than okay, hon."

"Met God, did ya?" Mr. French said, rocking the baby in his arms.

"For the first time, Mr. French." Neil drew a deep breath. "Huh! I'd like to say I get it now, but I'd be lying. He's so much more than I had imagined. I suppose it'll take quite awhile to sort out."

The crease between Mr. French's eyes deepened. "Sounds like my wife. Her reaction was about like yours when we found ..." Mr. French stopped himself.

Neil smiled. "When you found … Pete?"

"Who, Daddy?" Teri said.

"A man set aside by God for a special purpose, hon. You'll meet him one day soon."

Mr. French's eyes became as big as saucers. "How do you know about Pete?"

"I saw him." Neil climbed to his feet, his expression was a mix of excitement and disbelief. "God showed me the moments before … I … before I—"

"Killed all those people?" Mr. French's face was harsh.

Neil looked down at Teri. "Honey, you want to see Mommy?"

She lit up.

"Go on, then."

"Yippee!" Teri said, as she hurried away.

Neil gingerly took the baby from Mr. French. "Thank you for taking him from me. My mind was …"

"Sure," snapped Mr. French.

Neil flinched from the man's harsh tone. "You asked about Pete. Do you want to know, or shall I—"

"No. No, continue." Mr. French had a wall of anger raised, and Neil didn't know if more words would do any good.

"Pete was the only survivor of the *Princess*, Mr. French. But, of course, you already knew that." The baby fussed, and Neil rocked him back to sleep.

"Yes, I knew. I found his life-pod. The

question is, how did you know?"

"I saw him," Neil said, dismayed at his own words. "God showed him to me—this fifteen-year-old kid—preaching up a storm before—"

"You killed all those people." Stuck in his anger, Mr. French seemed to be looking for every opportunity to take Neil to task.

"He didn't kill everyone, Mr. French," Carl said from the doorway. "He let one escape-pod go. So now we know. The lone survivor was Pete, huh?"

Mr. French turned, his brow tightening as he considered Carl. "What do you know of this?"

Carl stepped into the room. "I flew Neil's wing, remember? When faced with shooting down that escaping pod—*Pete's* escape-pod—Neil couldn't do it. It was just one little pod, ... one life, ... but Neil couldn't pull the trigger. I saw, and I ..." Carl thought for a moment. "Humph. ... I *thanked* God. All these years, and I had forgotten that I had thanked God. Wow!" Realizing the significance of that simple act, Carl's eyes welled up, his chin quivered, and he glanced away to wipe moisture from his cheek.

With a thin, calculating scowl in his eyes, Mr. French looked from Carl to Neil, glanced back toward the hallway, and looked at Neil and the baby again. "You two planned this nonsense. You're both playacting to get me to believe you've come to Christ; that you're good guys. Do I seem that naïve?" Shaking his head, he walked away, and out of the room.

"He'll need time," Carl said, turning back to Neil to coo at the baby.

"You thanked God?"

With a slight nod, Carl half shrugged.

"So I had a latent Trog at my wing," Neil said, pleased to have heard this new revelation. "Will the wonders never cease?"

"Hmm. I guess you did, and … I hope they never do."

Neil handed the baby to the attentive Carl. "So, what were you doing on Atheron? I can't believe you showed up when you did," he said, as the two headed into the hallway.

"Are you kidding?" Carl said, gently bouncing the baby in his arms. "I thought you knew. Paladins are everywhere on Atheron. The church has gone underground, and—"

"The church was already underground."

"Okay, … *more deeply* underground. There is a pipeline to Hastings, Baldwin, and on to Calyx. I was sent into Seychelles to assess the situation there. Imagine my surprise at finding you in the middle of yet more gunplay."

"Well, I—"

"Five years," Carl said, as they stopped in front of Ramona's room. "Why do I continually find you in the middle of shootouts?"

"I'm just glad you do."

"Huh?"

"Umm, not in 'shootouts,' … the finding me part. Speaking of which, why is that always the case, Carl—your being there?"

"Cap, I've always got your wing. You know that. But I do need to get back to Atheron. I and a few other Paladins still have a job to do."

Neil grinned even more. "Captain Ogier, if you will tell me why you keep popping up, the ship is all yours."

Carl's smile was filled with pride. "It's like I said, Cap. I've got your wing. Per my request, our assignments always parallel."

"Well that explains the last five years."

"Does it?" Carl winked, handed the baby back to Neil, and turned to head up to the bridge, bounding three stair rungs at a time.

Neil passed his hand over the sensor, the door opened, and he stepped in to find Ramona asleep; her father standing at her side.

Wide-awake and sucking her thumb, Teri lay nestled in the crook of her mother's arm.

"You want to stay with Mommy longer?"

Teri beamed. "Can I?"

Neil gave a slight nod. "Your being here might do her some good, but be quiet and let Mommy rest."

Jean, sitting nearby, peaceably embraced by *Celestria's* avatar, was herself napping. The woman hadn't left her daughter's side since she'd come aboard, and Neil knew she was exhausted by the whole ordeal.

Celestria's smile said she knew Neil had finally come to grips with grace.

Of course she knew.

Nothing got past the ship.

Ramona's eyes opened a crack and she weakly reached out to take Neil's hand. Then she cocked her head to see him more clearly. "Oh, my. That's a nice look for you."

Neil glanced down at his dirty clothes. "Sorry, hon. I haven't had time to change."

She smiled. "I wasn't referring to your clothes. I was talking about your new heart. It fits you perfectly."

Tears suddenly flooded his eyes again. He leaned close to let his cheek caress hers for a long, gentle moment. "I love you, my wife," he whispered. "I always will."

At peace, she smiled and patted the bed next to her.

Neil laid the baby in the crook of her arm.

Ramona gently kissed the child's head and noticed the object in Teri's hand; the cake topper. Taking it, she looked at it carefully, and smiled a little more. "You shouldn't play with this, hon. Let's let Daddy put it back, okay?" she said, handing the figurine to Neil, then she drifted off to sleep.

Neil kissed her cheek and pulled back, glancing fleetingly at the topper; then he looked again. It had been completely restored; no crack or seem could be found at all; and without effort, he understood. As a tear trailed down his cheek, he looked up and saw that Mr. French was staring at him, but his father-in-law's expression remained severe.

He glanced once again at Jean and Celestria,

and then went back out into the hallway. Mr. French fallowed.

"You can take us back now," Mr. French said flatly. "I have to see if Pete—"

"I'm sorry, Mr. French, but you can't go back."

His glare stiffened. "And why not? I have business that needs my attention."

Just then Carl trundled down the stairs.

"Look, Mr. French," Neil said. "Right now it's simply not possible. All of Atheron is on high alert. They've busted the church at Cornesh and have your sector completely locked down. We can't go back there. Not now. *Not* for a long time to come."

Carl stepped up to them.

Mr. French was seething. "Pete, wasn't with us. I've got to find him."

"Mr. French, I can find him for you. What's his name, and where will he be?"

"His name is Pete Ailton. He should be in the—"

"Ailton?" Carl said in surprise. "Twenty-year-old, sandy hair, sparse, thin, mousy little mustache?"

"Yes, that's him."

Carl laughed. "I can't believe *that* is who you were referring to. Don't worry about Pete, Mr. French. He's working the rescue operation in Hastings, and from what I hear; he's making quite a name for himself."

"Yeah?"

"Yes, sir. He and his small squad are driving the Coalition troops nuts, running interference."

"Yeah?" Mr. French beamed with outright pride for Pete.

"Oh, and by the way, he'll be leaving with me once we're done here."

"Yeah? To where?"

"Sorry. If I told you, I'd have to …, you know."

"Hmm." Mr. French glanced at Neil before returning his gaze to Carl. "I think I get … you two. I get a sense that everything is as it should be …" he sighed, "… but I still can't help being mad. There just seems to be something wrong with letting either you off Scott free, but I suppose God knows what he's doing."

"So," Neil said, "you accept this then?"

"Yeah … but I don't necessarily like it. You better treat my daughter right, or so help me …"

Neil passed his hand over the sensor and they all stepped back into Ramona's infirmary room. Then a new thought popped into his head. "Guys, if you'll excuse me, I'll be back in a minute. I need to jettison an old helmet."

"No, sir, not just yet," Mr. French said. "I want that helmet."

"Yeah? Why?"

The old man shrugged. "To remind me that all things were paid for in full … a long time ago. Maybe it'll help me get over the loss of my sister … and Pete's dad."

Neil studied the older man. "Or it could just

stir your anger."

"I'm mad at you … that's true … but God is telling me to get over it. For the sake of my daughter, and my grandchildren, I think I'll do as He says."

Neil glanced at Carl. "Now I see where Ramona gets her tender heart."

Carl's agreeing nod said Neil was probably right.

A light tap on the door, preceded its opening to let John Bauer in. "Is she okay," he whispered.

Without a word, Carl threw an arm over the Pastor's shoulder.

Neil looked at his still-sleeping bride, the children in her arms, both in-laws, his friends, and even Celestria—and thought about all that he'd been through. Coupled with Jesus, his view about everything had suddenly, and drastically changed.

God was indeed good, and now he knew that as true, feeling his heart beat with elation against his breastbone.

And then he saw his own reflection in the window—his smile, though honest, held a mix of irony and self-satisfaction.

So *this* is success, he thought, his smile broadening.

Oh!

Super!

Made in the USA
Las Vegas, NV
28 January 2024

85013008R00144